Saltwater Studios

Pittsburgh

SALTWATER STUDIOS

ANJ Press, First edition. February 2020.

Written by Amelia Addler.

Cover design by Charmaine Ross at CharmaineRoss.com

Maps by Nate Taylor at IllustratorNate.com

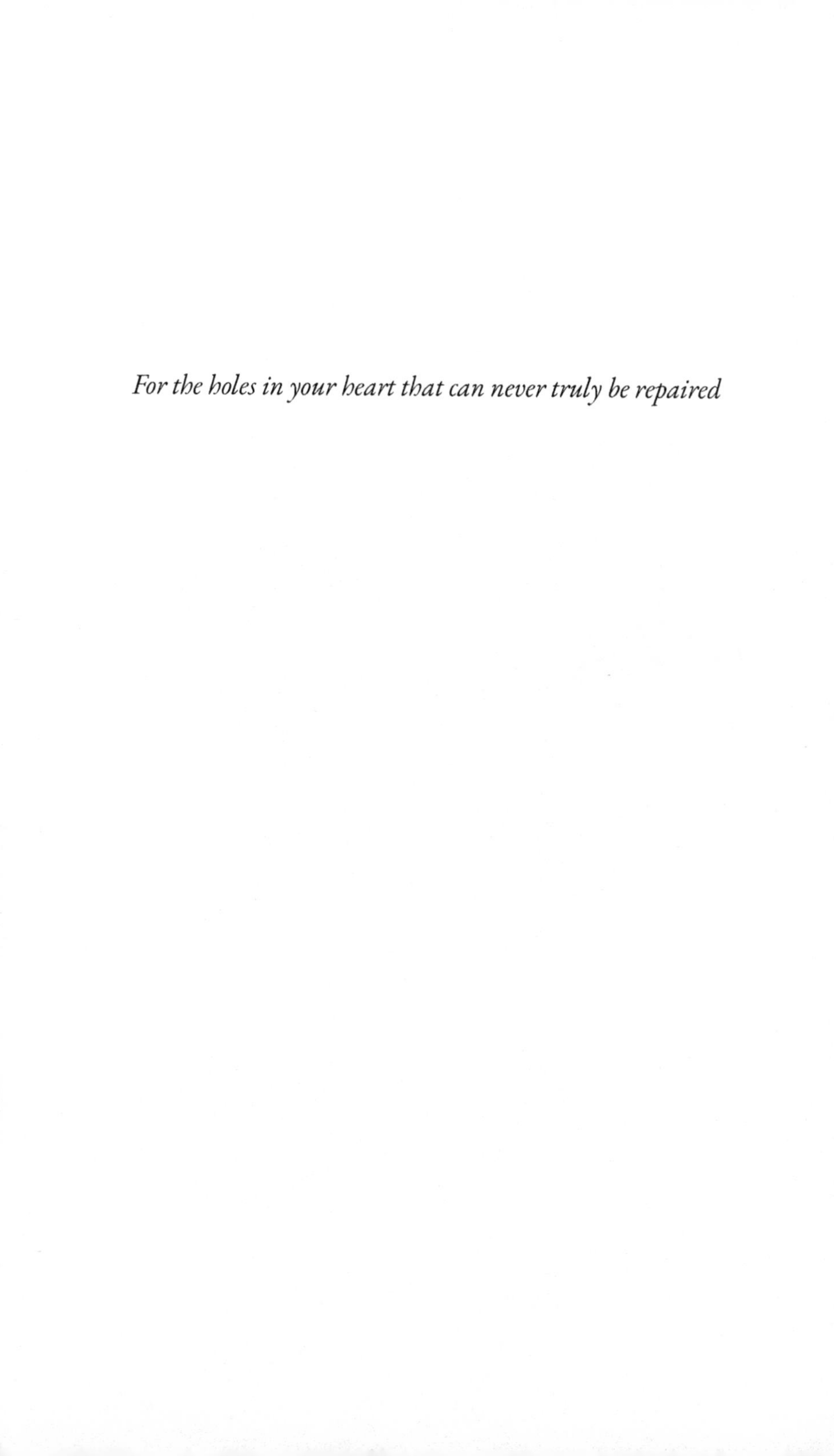

For the holes in your heart that can never truly be repaired

Recap and Introduction to *Saltwater Studios*

Welcome back to San Juan Island, Washington! In the first book in the Westcott Bay Series (*Saltwater Cove*), Margie Clifton got a second chance at life when her brother sold her his ocean front home and barn (for the fair price of $1). Margie, still trying to rebuild her life after her divorce from her husband Jeff, took the opportunity to turn the barn into an events space. She also planned to turn the house into a second home for her three adult children Tiffany, Jade and Connor.

Yet there was trouble in Margie's new paradise when a picture of a hit-and-run victim jolted her memory. Margie met the victim, Kelly Allen, over twenty years prior – when Kelly told Margie that she was carrying Jeff's child. But as soon as she appeared, she disappeared, and Margie never saw her again.

Thanks to the misguided help of the gruffly handsome Chief Deputy Sheriff Hank Kowalski, Kelly's daughter Morgan appears at Margie's doorstep. With no place to stay, Margie takes her in and quickly grows to love Morgan, who looks eerily similar to her own daughter Jade.

While Margie and Hank fall in love, Morgan and Jade strike up a friendship – much to the annoyance of Jade's husband Brandon, who would prefer to be left to tend to his fledgling DJ business.

Everything comes to a head when Jeff travels to the island for a surprise birthday party at the barn at Saltwater Cove. Margie confronts him and discovers that he did, in fact, father Morgan and that he does not care to make things right.

Brandon seizes the opportunity to manipulate Morgan into thinking that the entire Clifton family, including Margie, was out to get her and lie to her about Jeff. Morgan, already a hothead and still emotional from the loss of her mother, crashes the birthday party and releases an epic tirade on all of the party guests.

When it seems that Margie's dreams of a happy family are about to fall apart, Chief Hank gets Tiffany, Connor and Jade to hear the full side of Margie's story. They forgive her and accept Morgan as a new member of the family. Oh – and Hank proposes!

In *Saltwater Studios*, Hank and Margie plan their wedding while Jade struggles to finalize her divorce from Brandon. Morgan returns to San Juan Island with two goals: to start a photography business, and to discover the identity of the woman seen in a grainy video driving the car that killed her mom. Her biggest challenge is Luke, the annoyingly charming Brit who has more to his history than meets the eye...

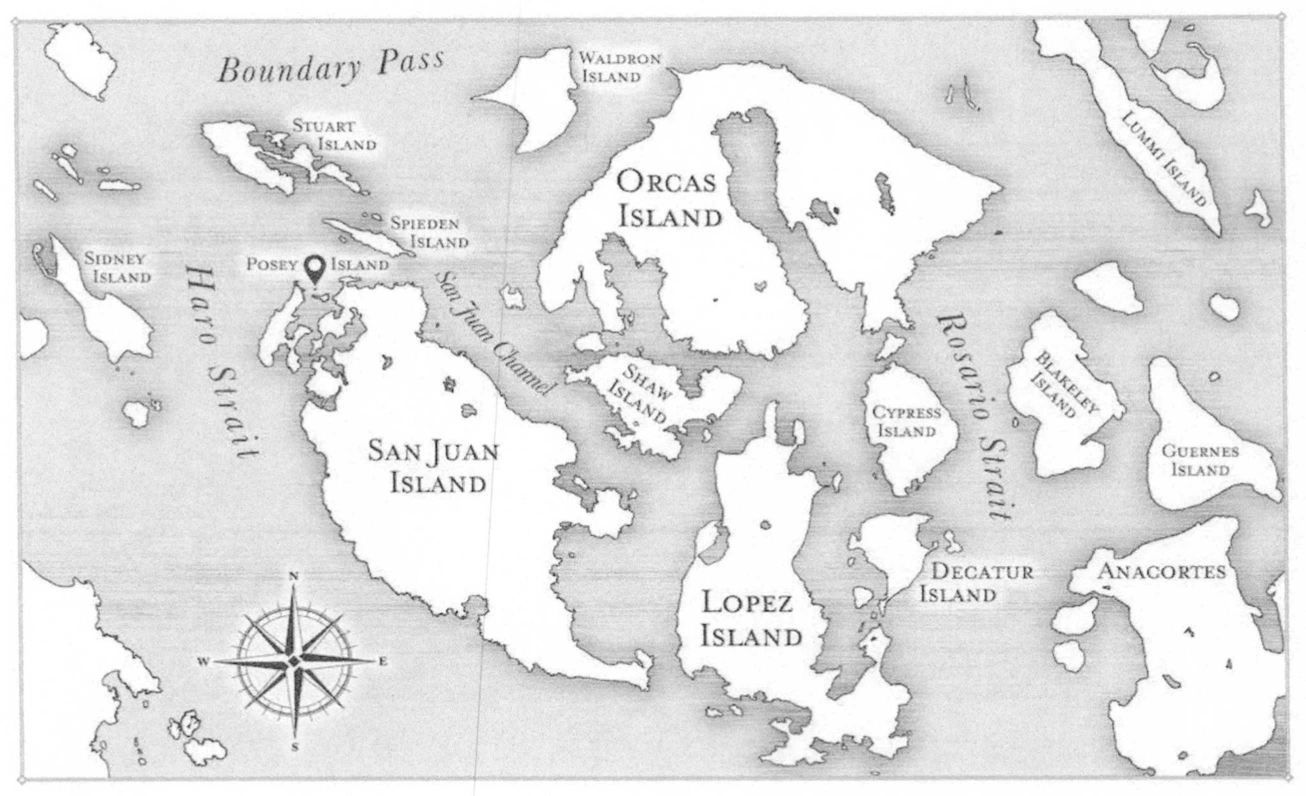
Boundary Pass
Waldron Island
Stuart Island
Orcas Island
Lummi Island
Spieden Island
Sidney Island
Posey Island
Haro Strait
San Juan Channel
Rosario Strait
Shaw Island
Blakeley Island
Cypress Island
Guernes Island
San Juan Island
Lopez Island
Decatur Island
Anacortes
N
W
E
S

Posey Island
Haro Strait
San Juan Channel
Westcott, Bay
Saltwater Cove
San Juan Island
Friday Harbor
Lime Kiln
Cattle Point
N
W
E
S

Chapter 1

The ferry felt like it was gliding through a cloud, cutting between the sky and the glassy reflection on the water. Morgan had to squint to make out the drizzled raindrops on the surface. It all looked a bit surreal, and normally weather like this would make her feel gloomy. But not today.

She was *finally* coming back.

Morgan spent the past year finishing her degree. It was tedious at first, but it gave her time to think about what she really wanted to do with her life.

For a blip in time, she considered becoming a police officer. She thought she'd become a detective and work on cases like her mom's. Chief Hank quickly changed her mind on that idea.

He rightly pointed out that Morgan couldn't handle blood and that she didn't want to be around a crime scene, let alone study the crime scene. Also, he destroyed Morgan's fantasy of verbally berating each criminal that she caught.

"That's not how our criminal justice system works," Chief said.

"You don't think that being yelled at is a good start to their punishment?"

He let out a grunt. "Actually, you're right. We've been doing it wrong all along. I'm going to retrain all of my deputies right away."

The overhead speakers crackled to life, asking drivers to return to their cars. Morgan felt a jump of excitement in her stomach – she'd soon be back in Friday Harbor. She told herself to remain calm. She was officially starting her new life and career, and she needed to be mature about it. It'd be unbecoming to race onto the island like a gleeful schoolgirl.

No, she was a year older and a year wiser. She knew what she wanted, and she knew how to get it. Kind of.

Despite trying to force a casual stroll, she was the first one back to the cars. After pulling her keys out of her backpack, she sat with them in her hand. It was too hot inside the car – did she need to open the windows? She felt sweaty and jittery – a mixture of excitement and fear. It was the same way she felt a few months ago when she sat her dad down to tell him her plan.

"Dad."

"Morgan."

She ignored his attempt to start joking with her. This was no joking matter. "I've prepared a PowerPoint about what I'm going to be doing for the next eighteen months."

"Is this a –"

"Yes, I printed out a handout for you. I'm going to walk you through it slide by slide."

He paused. "Should I be afraid?"

She ignored him and continued with her prepared remarks. "As you know, I have really been struggling with what to do after graduation."

"Right."

She clicked to the next slide. "Here you'll see that I applied to thirty-six jobs in various areas of industry."

He cocked his head to the side. "Industry?"

Morgan nodded, clicking to the next slide, which broke the details out in a bar graph. "Retail, food service, office work, and other. I wanted to get a good idea of what kind of entry-level jobs existed out there for me."

"Oh," he said, his eyes widening. "Alright."

She clicked again and a pie graph appeared on the screen. "As you can see, I received seven interviews, mainly in the food service industry. One was from a factory, and one for an office job at an insurance company."

"Right, that was the interview where you spilled coffee all over yourself on the way there."

She sighed. "Yes."

He laughed but didn't add anything else.

"Anyway. None of these felt like quite the right fit – not to mention that none of them offered me a job. So. I know that you'll think what I'm about to say is crazy, but over the next ten slides, I will show you my plan, including funding."

With another click, a slide that said, "Professional Photography" popped up.

She immediately looked at her dad to see the look on his face. Oddly, he didn't react at all.

"Before you say anything, I want to remind you that I have been shadowing – *interning* really – with a professional photographer for the past six months. At first, I started it just because I really enjoyed learning from her, but then, I started to think that maybe I could follow in her footsteps. On the next slide, you'll see the number of weddings that my mentor completed in the last calendar year, as well as how many non-wedding related jobs she took."

"This is amazing!"

Morgan turned towards him. "You really think so?"

"Of course! I don't know why you felt the need to put this whole thing together – I mean, it's great, but –"

Morgan interrupted him. "Because! I need you to know that I'm serious about this. And that I have saved enough money so I can get started, and I have a plan for the next eighteen months. I know almost *exactly* how much money I need to make to be able to support myself, and –"

"This is great."

Morgan paused. "Don't you want to see the rest? I feel like I need to prove to you that I'm serious."

"Hm," he said. "Prove to me, or to yourself?"

"To you, obviously. The *best* part of all of this is that Margie has a friend, Jackie, who has a photography business on San Juan Island. She does weddings at Saltwater Cove and all over the islands. Long story short – she and her husband do the photography and videography, but he was offered a job as a park manager at Yellowstone."

"Okay," he said slowly.

"So basically, they're moving away really soon, but they have all of these weddings booked out for the next eighteen months. She needs someone reliable to take everything over, and she said she doesn't want to upset all the brides she already has."

Morgan was talking so quickly now that her words were starting to slur together – she reminded herself to slow down.

"So Jackie wanted someone to step in and sort of act like they were part of her operation all along – you know, to keep the peace and not ruin her name in the photography business. That way, she can pick up work in Yellowstone and it will help *me* get exposure and reviews so I can start my own business. And anyway, long story short, Margie suggested that I be the one to step in, because she knows that I love photography...and Jackie said yes!"

"That's wonderful!"

"I know! I just have one more graduation party to cover with my mentor here, and then I'm going right up to San Juan Island to work with Jackie on her last wedding. After that I'm taking everything over! Almost all of her clients accepted me as the replacement, no questions asked!"

The smile faded from her dad's face. "So you're leaving pretty soon?"

Oh. Right.

In all of her excitement, she kind of forgot that her dad was looking forward to her moving back home.

"Yeah – I'm sorry Dad. I wish I could stay a bit longer, but..."

He shook his head. "No, of course not. I'll come and visit. I love San Juan Island."

Morgan nodded. "Yeah! You can visit anytime you want, and I'll come visit too, of course."

Her dad flipped through his printed handout. "Well honey – it looks like you have a *very* serious plan laid out here. I'm excited for you."

Morgan beamed. "Thanks Dad."

An announcement came through, telling drivers to start their cars. Morgan snapped out of her daydream and turned the key in the ignition.

On the one hand, she was glad that her dad took her seriously. On the *other* hand, it made her a bit worried – he was treating her like an *actual* adult, and that seemed...dangerous. She would be entirely alone. She had friends on the island, of course, but she was really on her own with this.

But! She had a new roommate – Jade! They were going to have so much fun living together. But not *too* much fun. Morgan needed to become a real photographer. She didn't really have a backup plan. Also, what could be more perfect than getting back to the island to nag Chief to work on her mom's case?

Morgan's car was the last one in her row, and she watched as all of the other cars cleared off of the ferry. Unfortunately, the car in front of her did not get the memo that it was time to go.

She sighed before tapping out a single, brief honk.

A head popped up in the backseat.

"Oh my goodness," Morgan muttered to herself. She watched as the driver scrambled from the backseat to the front seat.

Morgan rolled her eyes. So what if this person was a mess? She wasn't going to let it spoil her night. But at the same time, she didn't have all the time in the world and had places to be – she had to drop off her stuff at her new place, then get to a restaurant in Friday Harbor where Jackie was taking pictures of the rehearsal dinner. Morgan didn't want to be late – she needed to make a good impression.

She looked at the time – she wasn't sure when Jackie was getting to the restaurant, but she wanted to spend as much time with her as she could. The guy in front of her *still* hadn't started his car. Morgan felt the urge to roll down her window and yell at him, but with her luck, he'd probably end up being the groom for the wedding or something. She needed to behave professionally now that she was a "real" adult.

After another agonizing thirty seconds, the guy got out of his car. Morgan decided to pop her head out of her window and *calmly* see what was going on.

"Excuse me," she called out, trying to keep the edge out of her voice. "We need to get moving."

He turned around, clearly surprised to see her. "Oh! Hello there. I seem to be having some trouble starting my car. Do you have one of those – er, battery starters?"

Morgan crossed her arms. "No."

"Ah, of course not." He looked around and spotted an employee. "Hello! Excuse me Miss, could I bother you for a moment?"

Morgan let out a sigh. Her car was too close to his – she didn't think that she could pull her car around without hitting his bumper. And she was afraid to reverse at all – what if she accidentally launched her car into the ocean?

She didn't have time for this!

"How can I help you?" the attendant asked.

"Hi there, I'm Luke. Luke Pierce." He extended his hand for a handshake. "It's so lovely to meet you...Kathy?"

The woman smiled, accepting his hand. "Yes."

"I'm afraid I've become a nuisance to this young lady here, and my engine refuses to start." He turned around to face Morgan. "Truly my fault, I was at a concert late last night and afterwards offered my car's headlights to illuminate the beach party. You know how these things are."

"I don't," said Morgan flatly.

"Or maybe I forgot to turn them off when I got on the ferry...who knows?" Luke chuckled to himself. "Where are you from Kathy? Did you grow up around here, riding between the ports?"

She smiled – and maybe blushed a little? "I didn't, actually. I'm from Idaho."

"Really! Idaho! Such a beautiful state."

Kathy leaned in. "Thank you. Where are you from?"

"I'm from Radlett, just outside of London."

"Oh, London! You have a lovely accent."

"Thank you," he said. "I'm quite smitten with your American accent. How did you –"

"Okay," Morgan said, raising her voice a bit louder than she probably should have. "It's very nice meeting you all, but can we *please* get moving?"

Kathy snapped her head towards Morgan, the smile faded from her face. "Ma'am, I'm going to need to ask you to calm down."

Ma'am?

Luke smiled warmly at them. "I think my battery died and I'd appreciate your help ever so much, Kathy."

"I'll be right back." She disappeared into a stairwell.

"Well," Luke said, "I am so sorry about all of this. I'm sure Kathy will have me fixed up in no time."

"I hope so." Morgan replied, arms crossed. She knew she'd say something snarky to him if she was forced to continue chatting, so she decided to close her window and keep to herself.

She watched the clock closely – Kathy returned with a portable jump starter and attached the wires to Luke's car. That took four minutes. Then, between a bunch of flirting and blushing, they finally got around to starting the car. That was *another* eight minutes. After a few more pleasantries, he got into his car and drove off of the ferry.

Morgan put her car into drive and followed. They were the last ones off of the ferry. She told herself not to get upset and not to let it ruin her first day back – one schmuck wasn't worth getting upset over. She had places to go and people to photograph.

Chapter 2

"Well that was unnecessarily unpleasant," Luke said to himself as he drove through Friday Harbor.

How was he supposed to know that his car's battery was so sensitive? Come to think of it, there was a good chance that the battery needed to be replaced. Or perhaps something else needed to be replaced – plugs? Fluids? Bands or bits or bobs? Unfortunately, he had no idea how to do any of that, and he had even less interest in learning.

Oh well! There was no need to worry about it now. The car was running just fine. Well, mostly fine – there *was* that odd grinding noise.

It was fine. He got to his uncle's house quickly, but once he pulled into the driveway, he hesitated. Someone once told him that cars needed to run to charge the battery – or did it need to be off to *rest* the battery? He sat for a moment, weighing his options, but ultimately decided to leave the car running. It was safer that way, and he was going to be quick.

He hopped out, leaving the keys in the ignition, and knocked on the front door.

Nothing.

He knocked again, louder this time. "Hello! It's me."

Still nothing.

Luke went around the side of the house to the kitchen and peered into the window – it looked dark inside. Maybe he really wasn't home.

"I sincerely hope that you're not in there...because you're not going to like this," Luke said quietly.

He turned and walked towards the exquisitely landscaped succulent garden, its six foot waterfall quietly babbling. Luke squatted down and dug through the plants and embellished rocks. It took him about a minute to find the rock that felt different than the rest.

After checking that the key was hidden inside, he walked over to the kitchen's side door. He paused for a moment to make sure that no one was watching – it seemed like he was completely alone. The only sounds that he could hear were the wind blowing through the trees and the hushed sound of waves hitting the shore.

He slipped the key in the lock and opened the door.

"Perfect," he whispered. He replaced the key into its "hidden" rock and returned it to its spot.

He strolled through the kitchen and into the office, but didn't find what he was looking for; he then peeked into the library, but it wasn't there either.

Maybe it was downstairs in that enormous theater? Luke went to check, but there was nothing but gaudy reclining chairs and a lifeless popcorn machine.

The house was immense – he considered calling his uncle and just asking him where the wide-angle lens was hiding. There was a good chance, however, that he wouldn't want to tell him where it was, and that he wouldn't allow him to borrow it.

No, it'd be much easier to ask for forgiveness than for permission.

Maybe he kept it in his bedroom? It seemed like he had all kinds of junk in there that he never used – he just liked having expensive things in there to make himself look interesting.

Luke ran upstairs as the image of his car running out of gas flashed through his mind. He was unsure how much gas he had in the car; he had reason to believe that the gas gauge was not fully functional anymore. What he *really* needed to do was convince Uncle Brock to loan him a car. The man had far too many – what did he need with so many cars?

That was unlikely, though – as much as Brock wanted him to leave the island, he valued those cars more than anything.

Luke reached the top of the stairs and paused. It sounded like there was someone talking? Was it the TV?

He crept closer to the bedroom door and stopped once he was near enough to listen. It was definitely his uncle's voice – *and* the voice of a woman.

How riveting! Luke decided that it was time to make himself known and knocked loudly on the door.

"Uncle Brock! It's your favorite nephew!"

There was a loud sigh from within the room, and Luke listened as footsteps approached the door.

Brock flung the door open. "What are you doing here? And how did you get in the house?"

"I didn't know you had company, I'm *so* sorry. The kitchen door was open."

Brock narrowed his eyes. "Really?"

"Yeah, oddest thing. The gardener must've left it or something."

Brock looked confused for a moment before turning and walking back into his bedroom. Luke popped his head into the room, looking for the other person.

"I'm sorry about that," Brock said, picking up his laptop. "My little nephew stopped by unexpectedly."

"Oh! You're having a video chat," Luke said, letting himself in. "Sorry to interrupt."

"It's okay," Brock said evenly.

"You know," Luke said, seizing the opportunity of Brock being *forced* to be nice in front of this lady friend, "I just stopped by to see if I could borrow that wide-angle lens you were telling me about. It would be such a great help."

"Uh – I don't know that –"

"Oh! Here it is." Luke pulled it out of the large, black chest by the window; it probably held tens of thousands of dollars of video equipment, just collecting dust. "You don't mind, do you?"

"Well actually –"

Luke forced his way in front of the laptop's camera. "Hello! Who might this lovely young lady be?"

The blonde woman on the other end of the video smiled and waved. "Hi Luke! I've heard so much about you. I'm Andrea."

"Andrea! So nice to finally meet you. You're even more beautiful than Uncle Brock described. Though he's not the best with language, so you can't blame him."

Andrea laughed. "It's so nice to meet you too!"

"I can't believe that this is the first time that I've actually gotten to talk to you," Luke continued.

Brock cleared his throat. "Well Luke, you're always busy having fun."

"Yes," Andrea weighed in, "I remember some of the young ladies that you used to have over."

"Oh? Oh! *Right*." Luke shot a smile at his uncle. "What were their names again?"

Andrea tapped her chin. "Well, there was Libby, and Kimmy, and –"

Brock interrupted. "Feel free to borrow the lens. I hope it's useful to you."

Perfect. Andrea didn't need to know that it was actually Brock who used to have those "young ladies" over – not as long as he was willing to loan Luke the camera lens. Brock was welcome to use him as a scapegoat for his on-again, off-again girlfriend as long as Luke had what he wanted. He would leave. For now.

"Right. Thanks *ever* so much Uncle, I'll be seeing you later? And you Andrea – I can't wait to meet you in person."

She nodded. "Yes – definitely!"

"Uncle – would you like the door open? Or closed?"

"Open is fine. But please lock the front door as you leave."

"Of course."

Luke made his way back to the driveway, relieved to find his car still running. It was fun teasing Brock, and it was so easily done. The man wound up more easily than a child's toy.

And now that he'd met Andrea, he could probably leverage that whenever he needed. That, of course, plus Brock's worry that he would try to move in with him again.

The worry was unfounded, but Luke wasn't going to tell him that. It gave him access to things he actually needed, like his uncle's amazing video camera. And new lenses!

Brock wasn't known for his charity, so Luke reasoned that it was okay to come up with creative ways to cajole his familial affection. When Luke first arrived on San Juan Island, he was completely out of money and managed to successfully stay in his uncle's mansion for three entire weeks.

But Brock was adamant that he find his own place, and he became increasingly rude about it. That was how Luke first "borrowed" the video camera – he argued that it would give him a way to make an income and get out of Brock's way. He also correctly guessed that Brock didn't even know how to use the thing – it was another expensive toy he'd bought himself.

After that, Luke spent about two weeks living out of his car at a campsite near the ocean. That wasn't too bad, but it was still quite chilly then, and he didn't quite have the right clothes to stay warm. Once he'd made just a bit of cash, he took up at a hostel in town. That was rather fun, but some of his bunkmates had poor personal hygiene and it started to wear on him.

It was there, one night, as he lay trying to fall asleep amidst an awful rotten egg stench, that Luke decided it was time to get serious about making some money. As much as he liked San Juan Island, it wasn't the final stopping point for his trip, and it was increasingly obvious that Brock wouldn't loan him a penny.

Before getting to the island, he'd managed to drive the entirety of the US – from New Jersey all the way to Washington state. It was actually quite perfect that he ran out of money in such close proximity to a family member – even if that family member resented him for it.

The next morning, Luke decided to make the best of one of his uncle's connections. Occasionally, Brock employed a terrific photographer, Jackie, to take pictures of events or of his many cars.

Jackie was extremely professional, and she even managed to be friendly to someone as obnoxious as Brock. At times, Luke almost wondered if she *genuinely* liked him. It seemed too odd, though, so he chalked it up to her American hospitality.

He counted on that same American hospitality when he marched into Jackie's office with his portfolio and asked for a chance. He suggested that they could be partners – she would do the photography, and he would do the videography. She was hesitant at first, but admitted that her husband, who was currently making videos when needed, was overwhelmed and looking for a new job. After he showed her some of his work, she agreed to let her clients know that he was an option for events.

The rest, as they say, was history.

Actually – he was supposed to take some footage at a rehearsal dinner that night. The bride and groom didn't offer any additional payment for that, though – Jackie always got herself into these messes. She promised extra perks without charging extra fees. It was probably also why Brock liked her so much.

Luke decided he wasn't interested in working for free that night, and instead would get back home so he could plan the rest of his travels. His next goal was to drive across another country – maybe Canada? And he almost had enough money to make it.

Just a few more weddings and he'd be ready to leave.

Chapter 3

"Mom!" Jade yelled. "I just got a text from Morgan – she's off of the ferry. She should be here in ten minutes!"

"Oh! Okay – can I take over the kitchen for just a bit longer?"

"Of course!"

Jade got out of the way – she was really just a helper in her own kitchen that night. Her mom was the one making the fabulous dinner. She closed her eyes and took a deep breath – the house was filled with the intoxicating smell of fresh bread. If Jade were left to her own devices, she would probably just sit around and eat bread all day, every day.

In fact, thinking back, there were a lot of nights that she stayed in by herself, snacking in front of the TV. It wasn't *just* bread and junk food – sometimes she had pasta, too. Or any meal that was easy to make for a singleton. Having a roommate would be a big change – and hopefully a positive one.

"Is there anything that I can help with?" Jade asked.

"No sweetie, I think we're pretty much set! You just sit down and relax. This is so exciting!"

"How can I relax and be excited at the same time?"

"That's a good question," her mom replied, putting her hands on her hips. "I'm sure that you'll figure out a way."

Jade decided that she'd prefer watching and learning from her mom over sitting down and relaxing. In the past few months, she tried her hand at cooking a few times. Though she managed to make some pretty good meals, she was still too self-conscious to share them with anyone.

It didn't help that at one of their mediation meetings, Brandon casually told his attorney how awful of a cook she was.

"She tried using the grill once and almost caught the side of the building on fire. And every pizza she ever made stunk like goat cheese."

Even though she knew that he was purposely being venomous, it still hurt. She'd only made a goat cheese pizza *once*, and it was at his request! He never liked the toppings she put on and he suggested it; he also told her to buy a crust in the store because the ones she made from scratch always came out too burnt on the bottom.

And now his words echoed in her mind, as much as she tried to ignore it. She was terrified to let anyone try her cooking; what if they had to lie to her and say that it wasn't bad, but it was truly awful?

It was something she just couldn't face. Not yet at least. Her life was still too tumultuous.

"What kind of cheese is that?" Jade asked.

"Oh this? This is just mozzarella. But I always get the one in the medium sized package – you might be tempted to get the log, but it's too dry. So don't do that. And don't get the pre-seasoned one either. It can throw off the taste of the chicken parmesan."

Jade nodded. She needed to start writing all these tips down somewhere. "Got it."

She continued to watch her mom until the sound of a car pulling into the driveway broke her concentration.

"Mom! She's here!"

"Shoot, I can be out in just *one* minute."

"Okay, I'll go out now and help her carry her things in."

Jade couldn't remember the last time that she felt this excited – she pushed the front door open and practically ran to Morgan's car.

At first Morgan didn't notice her; she was bent over the center console, digging around for something on the floor of her car. When she finally sat up and caught sight of Jade, she startled.

"Oh my gosh!" she said, opening the door. "How long were you waiting there?"

"Long enough to see that your car is a mess!"

Morgan scrunched her nose. "If you think that's bad, you're *really* going to hate living with me."

Jade laughed and squatted down to hug her. "I'm so excited to see you! I've really missed you."

"Aw! I've missed you too! And *I'm* really excited to be here – except I just got stuck behind an idiot who couldn't start his car on the ferry, and now I've only got thirty minutes until I have to go to this rehearsal dinner."

"Okay then," said Jade, standing up. "Let's carry all of your stuff in, and then sit down for dinner. It's ready."

"Ready? You didn't have to make anything for me."

"Of course I had to! Well – I tried to. But then my mom heard about what I was planning, and she offered to help, and then..."

"Morgan!" Yelled a voice from the doorway. "Jade! What are you girls doing out there, come inside. Dinner's ready!"

Jade suppressed a smile. "Let's just grab a few things and carry them inside – we can get the rest later."

Morgan laughed. "I guess we don't really have a choice, do we?"

Jade managed to sling a heavy bag over her shoulder, tuck a pillow under her arm, and carry a large box. There were a few more things to carry in, but overall, Morgan didn't bring much with her. On the one hand, that was good, because their little rental house didn't have a ton of extra space.

Yet Jade was genuinely surprised by how little Morgan lugged around with her. Even last year when she came to the island, all she had was a backpack. And she hardly brought more than that this time, despite the fact that this was a more permanent move.

Jade was impressed – when she had to pack up her belongings from the apartment with Brandon, she couldn't believe how much stuff she'd collected over the years. Some of it was useful, but most of it was definitely not.

She struggled with throwing things away, though; she felt strangely sentimental about everything and told herself she'd pack it all up and decide what to do with it later. So now, the little storage space that their rental had was filled with boxes of mostly useless junk. Hopefully Morgan wouldn't mind.

They got into the house and dropped everything in the living room. Her mom practically attacked Morgan for a hug, and then refused to let her go.

"I am so, so, so, *so* glad you're here!" she said, squeezing her tightly and swaying from side to side.

"So am I," Morgan replied in a squished voice.

"Just stay still and eventually she'll lose interest and let you go," Jade said. "She's a lot like a black bear."

"A mama black bear?" Morgan suggested.

Her mom finally released Morgan. "Okay girls, that's enough! Sit down, please!"

"Oh my goodness Margie, this looks amazing!" Morgan said. "I'm really sorry though, I have to eat and run. I promised Jackie that I would help her with this rehearsal dinner tonight."

"That's completely fine!" She replied, pointing the girls to their seats. "Just sit down and enjoy!"

"Wow," exclaimed Jade. "I *love* your hair!"

"Thanks! You don't think it's too short?" Morgan's hand darted up to touch a piece, just above her shoulder. "When I was graduating I felt like I needed a change. So I cut off most of my hair."

"It looks awesome!" Jade reached out a hand to fix a piece that was sticking out. "And it's not that short. I feel like I've needed to do something with my hair, but I just can't decide."

Morgan nodded. "Don't worry. We'll find a new look for you too."

Jade smiled, then accepted a piece of chicken parmesan at her mother's prompting. She already felt better with Morgan around – Morgan had such an energy about her. It was kind of chaotic, sure. But wherever Morgan went, life went with her.

Jade felt like she'd been hiding for the past few months; the house was empty, quiet and dark. And she blended right into it.

"So – what's new with you guys? Margie, how's the wedding planning going?" asked Morgan.

"To be honest, we haven't really thought about it. I've been so busy with the barn – I mean, I did reserve a date so that we can get married. All of the other weekends are almost booked."

"That's great!" Morgan shoved a large bite of chicken into her mouth, struggling to chew and talk at the same time. "When is it?"

Jade cracked a smile. "Oh you know, in October. So *plenty* of time to plan everything."

"Time just keeps getting away from us," her mom said, shaking her head. "I'm sure it'll all be fine."

"I'm happy to help," Morgan said with a smile. "And *wow* – this chicken is amazing. I'm going to gain so much weight living here."

"It is a hazard of living so close to my mom," said Jade.

"What have you been up to Jade? I'm sorry I've not been texting as much – I was frantically trying to get ready to move. Any recent news from Brandon's lawyer?"

Jade took a sip of water before answering. "Not really. Brandon keeps arguing about every little thing."

"You have to support him, right? Through the divorce?"

Jade nodded. "I do."

"Do you think he's dragging it out on purpose?" asked Morgan. "I mean – you're paying for his lawyer, and you're paying for his living expenses, right?"

"Yes," Jade said with a sigh. She never expected the divorce to take so long, and she didn't know what else to say about it. She waved a hand. "New topic. How are you? How was interning with that photographer?"

Morgan stuffed her last bite of chicken in her mouth. "It was great! A really eye opening experience. I don't know if I'm ready to take over a photography business on my own...but here I am! It's now or never, and I need to make this work."

"Have you thought of a name for your business?"

"I have, but I wanted to run it by you first."

"Me?" Her mom touched her chest, feigning embarrassment. "I'm sure it's lovely."

Morgan set down her fork. "Well, I tried to think of a lot of creative names, but I kept coming back to the same one. And if you don't like it, or if it'll cause a problem, I don't have to use it."

Jade shot her mom a look. "This sounds serious. What is it?"

"I was thinking of calling it...Saltwater Studios. And I know that –"

"Oh, that's perfect!" her mom exclaimed. "I love it. And not just because it kind of sounds like Saltwater Cove's sister."

Morgan laughed. "I basically stole half of your name."

Jade waved a hand. "Don't worry about it. You guys are pretty closely linked anyway, and who knows? Maybe it'll be better for both of your businesses if people think that you work together."

"Of course we'll work together!" her mom exclaimed. "We women need to stick together."

"Well that's a relief," said Morgan. "Because I seriously cannot think of another decent name for it."

"Morgan, I don't want to be a bummer," Jade said, looking down at her watch, "but I think you need to get going."

"Oh my gosh! Yeah, I do. I've been having such a nice time seeing you guys – and this dinner! It was amazing. I'm so happy to be here. Okay, I need to run, but I'll be back soon. Probably. I mean, I think?"

"Just go!" said Jade with a laugh. "I'll still be up when you get back."

Morgan gave her another hug. "You guys are the best. See you soon!"

Morgan grabbed her camera bag and disappeared.

Jade turned to her mom. "I'm really glad she's back. I feel like we're going to have a lot of fun."

"I think you're right," she replied with a smile.

"What's *that* supposed to mean?"

Her mom shrugged. "Oh nothing! I just think that you two will make quite the cute pair. That's all."

Jade studied her for a moment, but couldn't figure out what she was getting at. She decided not to dwell on it. "Yes, I think we will!"

Chapter 4

The rehearsal dinner went pretty well; Morgan was stressed about officially meeting Jackie for the first time, but she was just as lovely in person as she was on the phone. They took some pictures of the restaurant before anyone arrived. For the rest of the evening, they focused mainly on taking candid pictures.

"Depending on what the bride and groom want, you may need to spend more time organizing posed pictures," Jackie told her. "But try to get as many candid photos as possible. Those are the ones that will end up in a frame – all the posed pictures end up looking the same. And they'll end up in a dusty photo album that's opened maybe once every couple of years."

"When do you gauge that?" asked Morgan. "For the couple, I mean – as far as what they want. Is it when you first meet them?"

Jackie nodded. "Yeah, I like to talk about it then. But I also have a meeting closer to the wedding to go over a schedule and their expectations."

Morgan felt like she should be recording everything Jackie said. "And what if they seem really determined to do things that seem like a bad idea?"

"Well, I try to show them a lot of sample pictures and narrow it down to a handful that they'd like. Also, by making a schedule, it's easier to outline what's possible and what isn't. If you have a very strong-willed bride though...well, you can see that for yourself tomorrow."

"Okay." A nervous flutter went through Morgan's stomach. Jackie was too polite to say anything negative about the bride, but it wasn't hard to tell that they would have their hands full.

The bride for this weekend – Helena – already snapped at one of her bridesmaids in front of everyone. Morgan could feel herself growing unusually shy; whenever someone's personality was over-the-top, it sort of scared her. She wanted to shrink away and hide under the table. Morgan wasn't even sure what exactly happened, but it was enough to scare her.

They got through the rehearsal without any more incidents, but that night, Morgan had a hard time sleeping. Though she'd seen her previous mentor Anna deal with some difficult brides, she didn't know how to mimic it; Anna was so experienced and collected. Nothing seemed to rattle her.

Morgan, on the other hand, felt like *anything* could (and did) rile her feathers. It didn't help that she felt like a total fraud; she knew how easily she could fail. It would only take a few bad decisions before she'd end up back home in Portland with a cloud of shame over her head.

It would've been nice to shadow Jackie for two or three more weddings, but it was impossible – she was moving to join her husband in just three days.

After the rehearsal dinner, Morgan got back to the house to find that Jade was still up.

"So? How'd it go? How's Jackie?"

Morgan flopped herself onto the couch. "It was good! Jackie is super nice. Like, *too* nice maybe."

"What do you mean *too* nice?"

Morgan sighed. "Oh, you know..."

She struggled with whether to say what she was thinking out loud or not. Once she said it out loud, it was a real thought and she could be held accountable to it.

But at the same time, without sharing it, it was hard to know if it was real, or if it was her being paranoid. It was just...

She'd tried telling herself that she was doing Jackie a favor by jumping in as this "other" photographer in her business, and not upsetting a bunch of brides when Jackie left.

But what was in it for Jackie? Was she really that worried about bad reviews ruining her prospects in the photography business when she moved? Was she just being nice to Morgan because she felt bad about her mom? Or...

No. Morgan couldn't say it out loud. She couldn't tell Jade that she suspected almost every woman on the island of being the woman who hit her mom with that car. Especially women who were nice to her.

It *was* too crazy of a thought.

Morgan cleared her throat. "I just don't want to disappoint anyone."

Jade shook her head. "You won't! You're going to be great."

When her alarm finally went off at six the next morning, Morgan was determined to present her best professional face. Sure, maybe she'd have to fake being a pro for a bit, but eventually she'd figure it out.

Probably.

She managed to quietly shower without disturbing Jade before slipping into a simple black dress (Helena's request). She triple checked that she had all of her gear before getting into the car. The wedding ceremony and reception were both on the west side of the island in Roche Harbor.

At the rehearsal dinner, Helena requested that they arrive at seven so they could get pictures of the sunrise with her wedding dress.

Jackie said that she would be happy to do it, but gently explained that sunrise would be its most brilliant on the east side of the island...and that it would occur just after five in the morning.

Helena mulled this over for a moment before asking, "So, can we do the sunset or something?"

"Of course!" Jackie said with a warm smile. "I think that you'll find it even more brilliant than the sunrise."

Nevertheless, Morgan wanted to try to get some morning shots and offered to come early. Jackie was appreciative and asked Morgan several times if she was sure she didn't mind.

"Of course!" Morgan said. "Nature shots are what I do best."

"I hate to leave you by yourself. But it'd be a huge help with Terri – my daughter. She's three, and she likes to sleep in as much as she can. So I won't have to get her to my mom's quite as early."

"I'm sure! I'll let you know if anything annoying comes up, but it should be fine."

"Well thanks Morgan!"

Morgan tried to channel the good feeling that their conversation gave her all the way to Helena's hotel room. Jackie didn't question her being on her own – so she must trust her. Right?

She decided to go with that for now and knocked on the door to the bridal suite.

Helena opened the door and smiled. "Oh! Hi. Mandy?"

"Morgan," she said with an overly enthusiastic smile.

"Right! Well help yourself to some coffee," Helena said, taking a seat on an overstuffed chair. "And if you could do some of the nature type stuff over here, that would be nice. I'm getting my hair and makeup done at eight – so you need to be here for that, obviously, but I don't really want anyone in the room right now."

"Okay!" Morgan replied, forcing a brightness into her voice that made her almost squeaky. She could feel her insides shrinking.

It was going to be a long day.

Morgan busied herself for the next hour with taking pictures of birds and harbor seals at the docks. The boats at Roche Harbor were quite stunning – much prettier than the average fishing vessel that she was used to seeing. She took her time getting the harbor from different vantage points and angles, even though she wasn't quite sure how much Helena would appreciate it.

It didn't matter – it was what the client asked her to do, so she was going to do it well.

Before eight, she returned to the room to find Jackie setting up.

"So what I'm doing now is getting pictures of her dress, the jewelry and the shoes – all that kind of stuff while they start her hair and makeup."

"But she said," Morgan replied, dropping her voice, "that she wanted pictures of herself getting ready."

"Oh of course – but we'll wait until she's completely done, then we'll have the makeup artist and hair stylist pretend that they're just finishing up. No bride wants a picture of her half made up face."

Morgan laughed. That was a good point – she didn't even know why she asked that. That's what they always did for brides in Portland. It was just that this bride scared her, so she was second-guessing everything she knew.

"Now we can take our time and find a place that has good lighting; it should be a spot that gives us an attractive setting for both far away and close-up pictures," explained Jackie.

Morgan nodded, but she found herself straining to decipher the angry tones coming from the other room. She was glad that the bridal suite had three separate rooms.

"Seriously, *where is he*? If he doesn't show up in the next ten minutes – I'm not even kidding – he's fired. I don't even care."

Jackie and Morgan made eye contact but said nothing. They continued taking pictures as Helena became increasingly angry. It sounded like her friends tried to console her, but she was reaching a breaking point.

"She's not talking about your husband, is she?" asked Morgan. She knew that Jackie and her husband worked as a team.

Jackie shook her head. "No – he's been down in Yellowstone for the past few weeks – and he had to go down for a lot of weekends to set things up. So I've been working with someone else to do the videography. Though this might be his last wedding."

"Because he's going to get fired?"

"No," Jackie said with a chuckle. "Because he's sort of a nomad. I think he plans to leave the island."

"Doesn't sound like the conscientious type," said Morgan in a quiet voice. "He's going to get us all eaten alive."

Jackie laughed. "Don't worry about it, we'll see what happens when he shows up."

As much as she appreciated Jackie's calm and collected demeanor, it seemed unwise. Helena was livid, and it wasn't even eight thirty!

Morgan could feel herself growing more and more nervous, which caused her to make mistakes. At one point, the thought flashed through her head that if she did a bad job, Jackie may not let her do any of the future weddings. It quickly became all she could think about.

Until, after about twenty minutes, there was a knock on the door.

"Come in," Helena called out.

Both Morgan and Jackie stopped what they were doing so they could listen. Jackie had a sort of half smile on her face that Morgan couldn't decipher; it seemed like this was the point where the yelling would *really* start. How could she find that funny?

"What do we have here," said a voice. "It seems like the *most* beautiful bride this island has ever seen."

"Excuse me," Helena said flatly, "do you mind telling me why you're over an hour late?"

Morgan positioned herself so that she could see what was going on. She recognized him instantly – it was the man from the ferry.

Of course. Somehow she knew she'd have to see him again.

Her stomach dropped – what if he *was* the groom after all? Was her intuition that good? That was one sure way to get herself fired from this wedding. Or was it? What did she say to him? Maybe she was nicer than she remembered?

"Late? I happen to have a beautiful shot of the sunrise for you, just as requested."

Helena's eyes brightened. "You do?"

He nodded. "Of course. I even caught a pod of orcas frolicking in the morning sun."

"They're here for my wedding day!" Helena turned to her maid of honor and they both squealed.

"What could be more lovely?" He unzipped his bag and pulled out a video camera. "So you stop worrying and start enjoying yourself. Everything will be perfect."

Helena nodded to him, a smile now stretched across her face.

Morgan hadn't seen Helena smile once today, yet now she couldn't stop. Even the night before at the rehearsal dinner, her smiles were less happy and more like a dog baring its teeth. In her defense, the restaurant only had one waiter working, when they'd promised four, but still.

He stepped into their room and closed the door behind him before giving Jackie a hug. "Good morning Jackie, my dear."

"Hi Luke," she said. "I'd like to introduce you to my protégé – Morgan Allen."

He turned to Morgan and extended a handshake. "Lovely to meet you Morgan, I'm Luke Pierce."

Morgan reminded herself to smile and shook his hand. At least he wasn't the groom. "Hi Luke, it's nice to meet you."

"Hang on a minute – haven't we met before?"

Morgan felt her heart rate pick up. Should she lie? It wouldn't be a good look to Jackie if she knew about the ferry incident.

"Oh, I don't think so?"

His eyes darted to Jackie, then back to Morgan. "Yes we have! I'm that nuisance who trapped you on the ferry yesterday, don't you remember?"

Dang it. "*Oh!* Right. I forgot about that."

He smiled, and Morgan got the feeling that he remembered *exactly* how she behaved. Oh well. It was too late to pretend now.

"How's your car?" she asked.

"A complete piece of junk," he said matter-of-factly. "But miraculously, still running. Now did I miss the ring set up?"

"I kept it laid out for you," said Jackie.

"Excellent, you're the best."

Luke spread out some supplies and got his camera ready. Morgan realized that she was clenching her teeth and reminded herself to relax.

"So Morgan," said Luke, "what brings you to the island?"

"Family," she answered. "And friends, I guess."

"How nice – family *and* friends."

Jackie went to talk to Helena and discuss the next shots; Morgan wanted to join her but felt like she had to at least be polite and reciprocate Luke's conversation. "How about you?"

"Oh, probably the same thing. Family. Well, not really – I drove across the US and by the time I got to Washington, I was completely out of money. But I had enough for a ferry ticket, and I've got an uncle who lives on the island."

Fascinating. "So, you're backpacking through the United States?"

"I suppose I am. Car packing? Is that something?"

"I thought that people were supposed to backpack through *Europe* to find themselves."

He turned to her and flashed a smile. "Who said I'm trying to find myself?"

Morgan felt her cheeks blush. He had a brilliant smile – she had to give him that. It was probably why he was able to talk himself out of trouble so easily. Well – that and his British accent. She'd only known the man for a day and already she'd seen him get his way twice.

How annoying.

"Just connecting the dots," said Morgan, trying to sound flippant. "Where did you spot the orcas this morning? I didn't know that there had been any sightings recently."

"The orcas?" He said, focusing his attention back on his camera. "Oh! Right. That wasn't from today."

Morgan narrowed her eyes. "What do you mean it wasn't from today?"

He shrugged, straightening himself out from his stooping position, before turning back to her. "Listen, I may have overslept. But I *do* in fact have a brilliant video of the sunrise – and of a pod of orcas. They just were not shot this morning."

"So you lied to her," Morgan said in a hushed voice. "Great. Now we'll all have to deal with her wrath."

Luke shook his head. "I didn't lie. I never said it was from this morning. I just told her that I'd gotten the video for her, which was true. She assumed the rest."

"Convenient."

He winked. "Don't worry, she won't figure it out. Unless she gets together with everyone else that I've made videos for in the last few months – and they all decide to compare sunrise shots."

She didn't even know what to say – not only was he late, but he also had no professional integrity!

"Are you really only going to include pictures that you took today? Even though it was unpleasantly foggy?"

"Of course!" said Morgan. "Because that's what she wanted, and that's what I did, and I stick to my word."

"Alright, I stick to my word too. But this is a woman who demanded footage of the sunrise on the west side of the island.

I don't know that she'll forgive the fog, even if she *did* demand it."

"That's not the point," Morgan replied in a raspy whisper.

"Right. Well, sometimes it pays to make things a bit nicer than they are in real life."

Morgan picked up her camera. "I think I'll go and check what Jackie is working on – we'll be doing the hair and makeup shot soon. Unless you have some extra footage of that too."

"*That* she probably would notice," said Luke. "But I like where your head's at."

Morgan chose to ignore him and join Jackie in the other room. She imagined a lot of challenges in starting this business – but she never imagined that she would have to work with someone like Luke Pierce. If only her troubles with him stopped on the ferry.

It didn't matter, though. She had to keep going, no matter what – even if the brides made her nervous and her hands got shaky and her voice was sometimes too high pitched. This was her dream and she had to do everything she could to give it her best shot.

No matter how annoying the videographer was.

Chapter 5

After gathering the jewelry and shoes, Luke followed Morgan into the other room.

"So I'm just going to put this fan right here, and it's going to gently blow your hair so that the pictures look really spontaneous and fun," Jackie said, setting up a few last touches.

Luke admired Jackie – she was a talented photographer and she treated every wedding as though it were important. Luke found that interesting because to him, each wedding was as unimportant as the last – a dull affair of the same repeated traditions, with a fifty percent chance of ending in divorce.

When he brought up the divorce factor, Jackie liked to remind him that the bride and groom were having a stressful day – though the wedding day may be quite fun for the guests, it was often not terribly fun for the couple.

Luke didn't care about any of that – he wasn't bothered by grumpy brides or pushy mothers-in-law. It was simply not all that interesting. Soon they'd go and record another bore of a ceremony. Following that, a mediocre dinner punctuated with overly long speeches from person after person who loved the couple dearly, but had the public speaking skills of a five year old child at show and tell.

His favorite part of the wedding business was how shockingly easy it was to make money. Shooting the videos was dull, but he could normally have them edited in a handful of hours, and it seemed that he could name any price. People *paid*, and gladly so.

Luke hoped that perhaps Jackie's replacement might be more on his wavelength, but oddly, she seemed as sincere as Jackie.

What was he missing? Perhaps she could enlighten him. When it was time to follow the limo, he offered to give her a ride.

"Thanks, but no thanks, I'll drive myself," Morgan replied.

"Oh come on, I don't bite."

"I thought your car was barely functioning?" she said, slinging her camera bag over her shoulder.

He frowned. "You're right, perhaps *you* should give me a ride then?"

Morgan stared at him for a moment – clearly she wasn't expecting him to turn that around on her. He hadn't expected to either. It just popped into his head – actually, it was her own fault for setting a trap for herself.

"Alright, that's probably a better idea. We wouldn't want you to be late again."

Luke smiled. "The consummate professional, I see."

"I try." She opened the door and motioned for him to walk through. "After you."

"And so polite!"

They got to the car and Luke was surprised to see that it was almost as old as his. It didn't smell or make any sounds, though, so that was an improvement at least.

"Now Morgan – how did you get into photography?" he asked.

She shrugged. "It's just something that I've always liked. And recently I made the decision to get more serious about it."

"Interesting. What prompted you to make that decision?"

She buckled her seat belt and turned towards him. "Did you get yourself an invitation into my car so you could question me about my life choices?"

He laughed. "Not exactly, but now that we're here..."

She turned around to back out of the parking spot. "Is it because you drove the entirety of the United States and you still haven't found yourself?"

Luke had to stop himself from immediately replying "no." A smile tugged at the corner of his mouth. Maybe he was wrong about weddings – maybe *everything* about them wasn't boring.

"What makes you say that?"

She reached forward to turn on the radio. "Just a vibe that I'm getting from you. I've just met you, but you seem very interested in my hopes and dreams."

"I didn't know that taking pictures of women in tight white dresses was your dream. And you never mentioned anything about your hopes."

She frowned. "It was implied."

"Well, the vibe that I'm picking up from you," he continued, "is that *you're* trying to find yourself, and you're projecting that onto me."

Morgan was quiet for a moment before responding. "No. I'm not trying to find myself."

"I don't believe you."

They pulled into a parking spot at the church and Morgan hopped out of the car. Before closing the door she leaned down and said, "I'm trying to create something. That's different."

Before he could respond, she closed the door and walked into the church.

He sat there for a moment trying to gather his thoughts. Where on *earth* did Jackie find this woman?

As much as he wanted to keep talking to her, it was time for his videography duties to come into play. He had to make sure that the audio in the church would work, and that his view wouldn't be blocked by the endless sea of friends' and relatives' cell phones.

He managed to capture every dull moment, and after the bride and groom left the church, they were whisked away in the limo to get their pictures taken by the sea. Jackie had a few favorite stops where she liked to take everyone to get their photos. She had a great eye, so Luke went along with whatever she said, and both the pictures and video turned out wonderfully. Regrettably, Morgan was one hundred percent focused on working and did not want to chat.

It wasn't until they got to the reception that he was able to set up his camera in view of the dance floor and sweetheart table. Then he was off to find Morgan, but unfortunately, she was busy taking pictures of the flower girl, who was delighted to find the dance floor completely open for her.

They then sat through a slew of predictably disappointing speeches before dinner was finally served.

"How are things going for you? Is this your first time on San Juan Island for a shoot?" asked Luke as he settled in beside Morgan.

Morgan had just taken a big bite of bread, but it didn't stop her from responding. "Yeah, this is my first shoot. And it's going well! Really well. I hope the rest of them are like this."

"They will be," said Jackie. "You're doing great."

"Thank you. That really means a lot. And again, I can't tell you how much I appreciate that you trust me to take over all of your current clients."

Jackie chuckled. "Of course! You're a lifesaver. When Margie told me she had someone, I knew they had to be good. She's worked with everyone on this island."

Morgan smiled. "Margie is one of the nicest people I know. If not *the* nicest."

"She sounds lovely!" interjected Luke. He knew that if he didn't say something soon he would be completely boxed out of the conversation. And he'd waited all night to be able to talk to Morgan again.

"She is," said Jackie. "I don't think that we've done a wedding there together, Luke. But she runs Saltwater Cove – you've probably seen some of the pictures I've done at the barn there."

Luke nodded. "Yeah – it's gorgeous. I look forward to shooting a wedding there."

"I thought Jackie said that you would be leaving the island soon?" Morgan said with scrunched eyebrows. "To continue your...self-discovery."

"I'm not really sure," replied Luke.

"Having some second thoughts?" asked Jackie, leaning back in her chair. "I had to *beg* you to do this wedding. I thought that it was going to be your last one, and then you were running off to drive across Canada?"

"I was," he said, taking a sip of water. "But it seems like my car might be on its last legs. It would be very irresponsible of me to leave before getting it fixed. Or maybe even replaced."

Jackie let out a little squeal. "Does this mean that I can tell my clients that you will do their weddings after all?"

"Yes Jackie, it does."

She clapped her hands together. "Okay, perfect! I'll let them know first thing in the morning. This is going to be awesome! And now you've got someone on your team, Morgan."

"Yeah, that's great." She smiled graciously before taking another bite of food.

Luke didn't buy her act for a second, but it didn't matter. He had the perfect excuse to stick around and prompt more of her barbed responses – he couldn't wait for the next wedding.

After dinner, Luke went back to fulfilling his duties as videographer. He could tell that Miss Allen wasn't terribly impressed with him, and he wanted to turn that around. Truth be told, he was decent at what he did. Sometimes he slacked on getting the videos edited, but he wouldn't do that this time.

At the end of the night, they said their goodbyes and Luke went home, even though normally on Saturday nights after weddings he would meet his roommates in town at the pub.

Instead, he went straight to his computer and uploaded the footage he'd taken that day. He was determined to get this video cut together within the week.

He couldn't risk disappointing his new partner, after all.

Chapter 6

Margie stole a look at the clock; she had fifteen minutes before her dinner guests arrived – the perfect amount of time. She poked her head into the dining room to make sure that nothing on the table was forgotten, but everything looked just fine.

Back in the kitchen, the chicken was happily frying away in the skillet; she'd never made this exact recipe before and was giddy with excitement that everything would actually be ready at the same time. On the menu for that evening were homemade biscuits, mashed potatoes, collard greens, and a new southern fried chicken recipe with cream gravy.

She came up with the idea for "Sunday Dinners" just recently, and she'd love for them to become a recurring tradition. What better way to do that than to make the first meal a pile of comfort food?

Promptly at six she heard a knock on the front door; she opened it to find Jade and Morgan.

"Hi!" they said in unison. Jade gave her a kiss on the cheek, and Morgan offered her a bottle of chardonnay.

"I didn't want to come over empty-handed," Morgan explained, "but I'm not a very good cook, so I googled what kind of wine would go with fried chicken. They said this helps balance the fat of the chicken?"

"That's very thoughtful of you," Margie said as she accepted it. "But I won't be having any, because I will fall asleep instantly."

Jade laughed. "She's not exaggerating. And right before she'd fall asleep, we might get a few frantic giggles out of her."

"That actually sounds pretty fun," said Morgan.

"Uh huh," Margie said, waving them inside. "Please, come in! I have some appetizers on the table. I'm just finishing up the chicken now."

They ignored her instructions to sit at the table and instead followed her into the kitchen.

"The smell in here is *incredible*," said Morgan. "Can I help carry out some of the dishes? Are these potatoes ready? And gravy?"

"*Look* at those biscuits!" Jade said, a hand covering her mouth.

Margie smiled – it never got old to have her cooking praised by her loved ones. Not that she needed the praise, of course. But it was nice.

"Yes, if you could carry these out, that'd be great," said Margie, loading their outstretched hands with plates. "But after that, have a seat. I want you girls to relax."

They walked off, chattering without pause, and Margie went to check on the chicken – the skin was a lovely golden brown – finally ready to come out! She carefully removed each piece using tongs, then poured the cream gravy over the entire platter. It looked even better than the picture she'd seen online.

Just as she set the dish on the table, there was another knock at the door.

She knew that knock. She called out, "It's open!"

"Hello beautiful," Hank said as he walked into the dining room. "What is this feast that you've made for us?"

He was about to hug her when she stopped him.

"My apron got a bit of oil on it," she explained, "and I don't want that to get on your nice red flannel shirt."

"Ah, of course," he said, giving her a kiss on the cheek instead.

"Chief! Long time no see!" Morgan said, giving him a hug.

"Hey kid!"

Margie stood for a moment and admired how he looked in his new shirt – she bought it for him, of course, but hadn't gotten to see him wear it yet. As expected, he looked extremely handsome. And like a big burly lumber jack, which she really liked...

"Mom?" said Jade.

Margie snapped out of her Hank-induced trance. "Yes sweetie?"

"Is there anything else that we need to get?"

"No – this is everything! But we're waiting on one more person."

Hank sighed. "I'm sorry – I told him not to be late, but he's just finishing up his shift."

"Who's this?" asked Morgan.

"One of Hank's new employees," said Margie. "He just moved to the island, so I thought it would be nice for him to get a bit of an introduction."

"Well I don't think that we should wait for him to start eating," said Hank. "I don't like the guy *that* much."

Jade laughed. "Really? Is he not very good?"

Margie scowled. "He's just kidding. He likes this young man *very* much. And we are not going to eat without him!"

Before he could protest, the doorbell rang. Margie startled from it – no one ever used the doorbell.

"I'll get it," said Morgan. "The sooner we get him in here the sooner we can eat!"

She returned a moment later followed by a tall young man. Margie smiled. She hadn't met him before, but he was *just* as she imagined – in uniform and all!

"Oh, hello everyone," he said somewhat sheepishly. "I'm so sorry that I'm late, we had to help with a gaggle of escaped pet geese that were running loose in Friday Harbor."

"Likely story Stevens," said Hank, shaking his head.

Morgan nodded, arms crossed. "Yeah. A wild goose chase. We *totally* believe you."

Jade let out a small laugh but said nothing.

"Stop it!" Margie snapped as she whipped off her apron and extended a handshake. "Hi, I'm Margie Clifton, it's very nice to meet you."

"Hi Margie," he said, accepting her hand. "It's nice to finally meet you. I've heard so much about you at the station."

"Everyone," Hank interrupted, "This is San Juan County's newest employee, Corporal Matthew Stevens."

He smiled and waved.

"Well Corporal," said Morgan, "why don't you have a seat so this meal doesn't go to waste?"

"Of course, I'm sorry," he said, sitting down next to Jade.

Excellent.

Margie sat down, careful to watch Jade's expression as Matthew settled in. Jade smiled, but seemed a bit frozen and didn't make eye contact with Matthew.

They went through introductions as they passed the plates around. Margie was happy to see that everyone served themselves large portions – it was a good first sign that the meal could be a hit.

"So Chief," Morgan said, setting down a chicken bone. "Please tell me that you hired more staff so that you could focus on my mom's case?"

Hank smiled. "Of course."

"Really?" Morgan turned to him, eyes bright.

"Well, not exactly. But I do plan to get him on your mom's case. Sometimes a fresh set of eyes can really turn things around."

"I'm sorry," said Matthew, "is there really a case concerning your mom?"

Morgan nodded. "Yes. We are creeping up on a year and a half of my mom's murder going unsolved."

Margie felt herself take a deep breath at the word "murder." She noticed that Jade flinched, too.

Morgan continued. "She was visiting the island with my dad when someone hit her with their car and left her to die."

"I'm so sorry," Matthew said.

"Thank you." Morgan paused for a moment. "And if you could figure out who did it, that would be a huge help. Chief, so far, has *not* done the best job."

Hank laughed. "That's no small order, you know."

Morgan laughed, too, and Margie let out a sigh. Margie didn't want to upset Morgan, but she also didn't want to scare poor Matthew away.

"I can't believe you haven't been able to identify the woman in the security footage," Morgan added. "Maybe *you* could look into it Matthew? Are you any good with technology?"

He nodded. "Yeah, you could say that."

"Did you do a lot of tech stuff in your old department?" asked Morgan.

Matthew shook his head. "Not exactly. But I used to be an electrical engineer. And I did a bit of programming as well."

"Jade does programming too," interjected Margie.

Jade nodded and smiled, but didn't say anything. Margie's heart fell. She hated to see Jade retreating further into herself. It seemed like it was much worse after the divorce, and no matter what she tried, Margie couldn't get her to talk.

"Oh yeah, Jade's a pro," Morgan said. "But how did you go from being an engineer to being a cop?"

Margie felt the thump of a foot under the table – it appeared that Jade delivered a discrete and swift kick to Morgan. Margie had to force herself not to laugh.

"That's a great question, and one that everyone back home keeps asking themselves," said Matthew with a laugh. "And I don't know. I went to school for engineering, got a job, worked there a few years. But it just didn't feel right. I wanted to do something more with my life."

"Like chase geese?" quipped Hank.

Matthew laughed. "Yeah, when needed. You wouldn't believe how vicious they were. One bit me pretty good." He pushed up the sleeve of his T-shirt to reveal an impressive bruise. Even Jade turned to look, eyeing the bruise and the rest of his arm muscles carefully.

"Geese are possibly the most aggressive inhabitants of the island," Hank commented.

"That's pretty funny," Morgan said, leaning in to examine the bite. "But I *think* what you're really trying to say is that you're going to find my mom's killer, because it's *exactly* what you got into this job for."

Another kick. Morgan didn't flinch, and Margie couldn't help it – she giggled.

"Of course, I'll do everything I can," said Matthew. "It really is the reason that I got into this line of work."

Morgan took a deep breath and leaned back in her chair. "Alright Chief, I guess I approve of your new hire."

"Thank goodness," he responded. "Because I was having my doubts."

Matthew laughed but Margie felt like it was time to step in.

"Okay you two," said Margie. "Stop picking on the new guy! What do you think of this chicken?"

"It's *fantastic* Mom," Jade said. "And these biscuits are unbelievable. Can I get the recipe from you?"

"Of course!"

"Maybe we can take turns with who hosts Sunday dinner?" Morgan suggested. "I think if we work together, Jade and I can pull off something like this. And by something like this, I mean about half as elaborate, but with just as much hard work. And probably more use of the smoke detector."

Everyone laughed.

"I think that's a great idea," said Margie. "And I'm sure that you would do a lovely job. Now Hank, it looks like everyone is finishing up. Can you please help me clear the table so I can bring out dessert?"

"I would love to, my dear. How about you stay here and relax and I'll clear the –"

"No! I need to add some finishing touches on the dessert. So you just – you just come and help me."

"Whatever you say," he said, standing up and stacking dishes.

They carried the plates into the kitchen, and as soon as they set the stacks down next to the sink, Hank swept her into an embrace and kissed her.

She kissed him back for a moment, but then pulled away.

"*What are you doing!*" she whispered.

"I'm kissing my beautiful fiancée who is a wonderful hostess, expert chef, and if I do say so myself, one hot lady."

Margie pushed him away. "What has gotten into you!"

Hank laughed. "What! I didn't get to even give you a hug when I came in, so I felt like I needed to make it up to you."

She couldn't help but laugh at him. He was adorably affectionate despite being such a big, burly man. If only the guys in the Sheriff's office knew this side of him – they would never stop teasing. And they already teased him quite a bit.

"Listen," she said in a hushed voice. "I think we should leave them alone for a bit."

"Why?" asked Hank. "So Morgan can scare Stevens off the island?"

"No, because I think..." Margie looked around to make sure that no one had come close to the kitchen, "that Jade might like Matthew."

"Really? What makes you say that? She hardly even spoke to him."

"Exactly!" Margie pointed a finger. "She's always shy around new people, but this was different. I don't know if you've noticed, but Matthew is a good looking young man."

"I have not noticed," said Hank. "But if you say so."

"I do. And I know that Jade has been down since the divorce. Do you think he's a nice guy?"

Hank shrugged. "I think so, but I can't be sure. Not yet. But so far he seems like a normal guy."

"I have a good feeling about him," said Margie. "There's something in his eyes. I trust him."

Hank leaned back, crossing his arms. "What you saw in his eyes was the terror of facing Morgan's questioning. Nothing else."

"No, it wasn't that!" Margie said. "He just seems really... genuine. I guess we'll see."

"Yes, I guess we'll have to wait." Hank picked up the dessert platter. "Did you want me to drop this dessert on the floor or something so that you have to make a new one, or...?"

"No, let's just hang back for another ten minutes or so. I'll tell them that I'm letting the dessert set."

"Does this have to set?"

"Of course not, but they don't know that."

"Okay," Hank said, setting it down. "But one more thing."

"What?"

He wrapped his arms around her, pulling her in tight. "You have to kiss me at least once before I let you go."

Margie laughed and shook her head. "Oh fine, if you insist."

Chapter 7

The first Sunday dinner was a success for Morgan; not only did she manage to scare the new deputy a bit, but she also convinced Margie and Jade to go on a hike with her the following weekend.

On Saturday, Morgan had a wedding to shoot on Orcas Island, but the weather was so perfect that she couldn't resist squeezing the hike in beforehand. She popped out of bed promptly at five, mainly to be sure she had enough time to get Jade out of bed.

"Oh Jade! Wake up sunshine!" Morgan called out as she flickered the light on and off in Jade's room.

Jade grunted and pulled the covers over her head. Morgan had always been a morning person, and for some reason, she assumed that Jade would be too. So far, however, all evidence in their tenure as roommates pointed to the opposite.

Morgan frowned at the lumpy figure on the bed. "Oh come on! You said you wanted to go for a hike to see the sunrise."

"I meant *theoretically*," said Jade as she sat up. "I didn't know that you would drag me out of bed like this."

Morgan giggled. It was so rare to catch Jade so cross.

"No you did, remember?" Morgan said brightly, pulling open the curtains. Unfortunately, it was still dark outside. "I said I was going to get these incredible views of the east side of the island, and your mom said –"

"I know, I know," Jade said with a groan. "She said it would be great for us to go with you and get some of the fresh air."

"And you agreed!"

"I didn't actually say anything," Jade protested. "So I'm going back to sleep."

Morgan sighed and put her hands on her hips. "I thought you just weren't saying anything because you felt extra, super shy around Corporal Stevens?"

Jade emerged from under the blanket again. "That's not true! I just – I don't like talking around strangers."

"Strangers? All of them, or just the tall, handsome, and broad shouldered ones?"

"*Stop*," Jade groaned, hiding her face in her hands.

Morgan hopped onto the bed and wriggled next to Jade. "I'll stop if you agree to come with me."

"Fine," Jade said, her eyes still shut.

"Yay!"

"How long do I have to get ready?"

Morgan looked at her watch. "Since we've been debating you getting out of bed for so long, you have seven minutes."

"Seven minutes! How long is this hike going to take?"

"Come on! Brush your teeth and I'll pick out an outfit for you."

Jade slowly rose from bed and shuffled to the bathroom. Morgan pulled open a few of the dresser drawers until she found some clothes that would be appropriate for the weather.

It took Jade fourteen minutes to get ready – double what Morgan said she was allotted. It was fine though, because Morgan had actually planned for Jade to take a full thirty minutes – now they were ahead of schedule!

They met Margie at the Cattle Point Lighthouse. There were a series of trails there, including one along the shore that

Morgan paced many times by herself. What started as an obsession with being close to Brock Hunter's house turned into a genuine love for the area. Of course, Morgan was tempted each time to trespass again, but Hank sternly warned her enough times that she was able to resist. He said that any further meddling could ruin the case – and they were doing everything that they could to get information.

The sun already began its ascent as they debated which way to go; Morgan was delighted when they agreed with her recommendation to hike west. It was a hard sell, because the trail grew narrow at points and skirted the edge of the cliffs. Morgan wasn't great at guessing heights, but she thought the cliffs at points were a hundred feet above the beach.

When she was alone, she relished how the windswept dunes absorbed the sound of her footsteps; further into the trail, the taller grasses blew delicately in a sort of ancient dance. When the trail neared the edge of a cliff, Morgan loved to stand and listen to the water breaking against the rocks. The beaches were always littered with timber, worn white from the sea. They piled up on the shore and Morgan resisted the urge to run down and collect branches. What she would do with them she had no idea – but the smooth wood appealed to her nevertheless.

Today, however, it was difficult to hear the waves or admire the wind breezing through the grasses over the sound of Margie's terror.

"Oh my goodness!" yelled Margie. "Should we all be tied together or something? In case one of us slips?"

Morgan peered over the edge of the cliff, strangely enthralled by the fact that a single misstep could mean the end. It was terrifying, of course – but exciting.

"No!" replied Morgan. "Just focus on the trail ahead of you and you'll be fine."

Jade paused and peered over the ledge. "It doesn't look like a swift death. It looks like you'd fall, and keep falling, and hit a bunch of stuff on the way down, and possibly still be alive when you hit the beach."

"Don't be so morbid," said Morgan. "Look at the colors of the sky! Have you ever seen anything so breathtaking?"

Jade looked up and smiled. "You're right – it is gorgeous."

"Keep your eyes on the trail!" Margie barked. "Because if either of you go down, I'm going down after you!"

Morgan stopped and turned to face them. "It's *really* not that dramatic. If you're scared, come over and be on my right."

"That's a good idea – Jade honey, go stand next to Morgan."

"I'm not a baby! I'm perfectly able to keep myself from –" Jade's left foot slipped, sending a rock careening down the side of the cliff.

Margie screamed and grabbed her, and Jade burst out laughing.

"I'm just kidding Mom!" Jade said, skipping ahead of them a bit. "And you're right Morgan – it is unbelievably beautiful up here."

Though there was a special place in Morgan's heart for grumpy Jade, she was glad to see that normal Jade was back. They managed the rest of the hike without any further incidents, and Morgan snapped a few pictures that really captured the beauty of the island.

She'd never admit it, but she got the idea from Luke. Unlike him, she wouldn't pass off the images to some unsuspecting bride and lie, saying that they were from her wedding day. But it wouldn't hurt to have these pictures on her website for potential clients. Or, she could even sell prints.

The hike was lovely and Morgan wished that they could go further, but she wanted to get back to the house and get ready for the wedding shoot. Plus, they needed some time to try the new coffee place that Jade *insisted* on taking them to.

"It's called Oyster Coffee. They roast all of their own beans and have drink specials of things from the islands – like chocolate and lavender. We can grab a little breakfast, too!"

"Anything to get us away from that cliff," said Margie. "Are all of your hikes this dangerous? If so, then you should never go on them alone again!"

Morgan laughed. "It's really *not* that dangerous. And no – this is probably the highest one. Next time we can hike north; the trail goes right along the water. Sometimes there are sea lions sunbathing on the rocks."

"That sounds much less stressful," Margie replied.

"Less stressful, yes," Morgan said. "But much stinkier. Have you ever smelled a sea lion?"

"I can't say that I have!" Margie said with a laugh.

They got to the coffee shop right after seven, and Morgan was surprised to see how crowded it was. Standing at the end of the sizable line, Morgan started to feel nervous that she may not have enough time to get home, change, and catch the ferry to Orcas Island.

The group ahead of them was four young women, all with long, blonde hair and dressed as though they'd just walked out of a hiking catalog.

"Maybe we should just go," Morgan said in a low voice. "Somehow I don't think these girls will be ordering black coffee. Probably something with whipped cream, and sprinkles, and involving a blender..."

"Oh, stay! The line is going quickly," replied Jade. "You'll see – you'll love it!"

Morgan frowned. She didn't want to ruin Jade's fun, so instead, she weaved through the crowd to grab a menu from the front counter; at least that way they could be prepared to order when they finally got to the front.

"Fancying a cup of tea?" said a voice.

Morgan froze. She knew that voice. Of *course* he would be here. She looked around but didn't see his face.

"Now I normally wouldn't support a line jumper, but for you I'll make an exception."

She turned back to the counter and saw Luke standing there in a green apron that read, "Kiss the barista."

"Oh – hey. I didn't see you."

"Anything look good to you? You know, I can make your wildest dreams come true – pumpkin spice, toffee, whipped cream –"

A woman behind Morgan cleared her throat. She turned around to see that was one of the hiking models. "Excuse me – I think you need to get to the back of the line. We were next."

"I'm so sorry – I wasn't cutting, I just wanted to get a menu," Morgan explained as she backed away.

"Nonsense," said Luke. "Miss, surely you and your lovely friends wouldn't mind if San Juan's premier photographer grabbed a quick drink as you're making your choice? After that, you'll have my *full* attention."

A smile spread across her face. "Well, since you asked so nicely."

He winked at her. "I always ask nicely."

Blech.

"It's really fine," Morgan said over her shoulder as she rushed back to Margie and Jade. Was there *anywhere* she could go on this island without having to deal with Luke Pierce?

Margie gave her a puzzled look when she returned. "You caused quite a stir up there."

"It's nothing," Morgan said, shaking her head. "Just a misunderstanding."

Jade smiled. "Do you know that guy?"

"Uh, kinda," Morgan replied, determined to keep her eyes fixed on the menu.

"Because he's still staring at you," said Jade. "And if I didn't know any better –"

"Hello ladies!" boomed Luke's voice. Somehow he managed to sneak up on them.

"Hello!" replied Margie and Jade in unison.

"Morgan, who are your delightful friends?"

All three of them were just standing there, smiling at her. Morgan sighed. "This is Margie. And this is Jade, her daughter."

Jade crossed her arms. "I'm also your friend. And roommate!"

Morgan nodded. "Right. And this is Luke Pierce, he's a videographer here on the island."

Luke eagerly shook hands with each of them. "It's so nice to finally meet you Margie, you're even more lovely in person than what I've been told. I cannot wait for my first wedding at your beautiful barn."

"Well thank you," said Margie with a blush. "Aren't you just the sweetest!"

Morgan realized that her jaw was clenched. She forced herself take a deep breath and release it.

"So are you going to be doing the videography for the wedding with Morgan today?" asked Jade.

Luke turned to Morgan. "I'm not actually, and what a crime! We have so many weddings in the next few months that we're working on together, how could I miss this one?"

"It must've been one that you turned down when you decided you were done being a videographer," said Morgan with a smile.

Luke took off his apron. "Well that just won't do."

"No really – it's okay. I don't think that this couple can afford your services on zero notice. And you're clearly busy here, so –"

He shrugged. "It's really fine. I only promised to help open the coffee shop this morning. I used to work here more regularly before my videography business took off. I was just helping today as a favor to the owner."

"Well that's quite nice of you," said Margie.

"Perhaps," Luke continued, "I can switch gears today and be your second shooter. I'm not a terribly skilled photographer, but it couldn't hurt, right?"

"I only have one camera," Morgan said quickly. "But thanks."

"Oh I have a camera," Luke said.

"And didn't you say," Jade added, "that you really need to get a second shooter to take your business to the next level?"

"No, I don't think so," Morgan stammered.

"That does sound like something that she would say," said Luke matter-of-factly.

"I really don't think that these ladies at the counter can manage without their soy vanilla bean mocha whatever's," said Morgan. "And I, on the other hand, am going to be totally fine."

"Nah," he shook his head. "We're going to make a great team today. Be right back."

They watched as he went behind the counter and said his goodbyes.

Jade leaned in. "Well, well, well. It seems almost like you were projecting about – what did you call them? Tall, handsome and broad shouldered strangers?"

"I was not, thank you. Luke and I are...professionally intertwined."

"Professionally *intertwined*," Jade mused. "That's one way to put it."

He reappeared at Morgan's side. "Alright, are you ready to go?"

"We didn't get any coffee yet," said Margie. "Do we have time to...?"

"Of course!" he said. "Just tell me what you need and I'll run to make it. On the house."

Margie and Jade placed their orders, but Morgan insisted on paying.

"I understand that you don't want to be in my debt, Miss Allen, but if we are to be partners –"

"We're not partners, Luke. We're – collaborators. It's very different."

"Of course," he said before going back behind the counter.

Morgan shot Jade a look and she took the hint – no more comments. The truth was that Luke was much better connected in the wedding business, even if he didn't care about it as much as she did. If he insisted on being her partner – er, collaborator, she wasn't going to stop him. She couldn't, in fact. Not if she wanted Saltwater Studios to have a chance.

He returned with their drinks in hand. "Shall we?"

"Sure," Morgan said, forcing herself to smile. "Let's go."

Chapter 8

Since Luke's rental house was near the ferry terminal, Morgan agreed to meet him there after she went home to change and get her camera. Surprisingly, she even agreed to carpool with him – but only after he pointed out that both of their cars may not fit onto the ferry.

He didn't know if that was true, but it worked. Luke wasn't used to women trying to avoid him. Not that he thought every woman was in love with him or anything; he just found that a bit of charm went a long way. And he wasn't sure what he did to offend Morgan, but it seemed it'd be interesting to find out.

And hey, at least her friends liked him.

He took a quick shower and changed before grabbing his camera on the way out. There was no doubt in his mind that Morgan would not wait for him if he were late, so he couldn't let that happen.

Not five minutes after he got to the ferry terminal, he spotted Morgan pull up in her car. He smiled and waved before jogging over – she offered a nod and unlocked the doors.

"Hey! Glad I found you. You know, I was thinking that I should probably get your phone number for situations like these – you know, in case we lose each other."

"Yeah – I guess that makes sense," she said as she pulled out her phone. "What's your number? I'll call you."

Bingo! "Good idea."

They exchanged numbers and then silence threatened to settle between them. Luke couldn't allow that.

"So how are the pictures coming along for Helena's wedding?"

"I'm done. I was planing on sending them to the bride and groom today."

"Oh," Luke shook his head, "I wouldn't do that."

"Why not?"

"How long did you tell them it was going to take?"

Morgan shrugged. "I was just following the timelines that Jackie had before. I think she promised a few select pictures two weeks after the wedding, and delivery of all of the pictures six weeks after."

"Alright. That's smart."

"But it was the only wedding I had to do, so I got it all done pretty quickly."

Luke felt excited that he knew something Morgan didn't know. "Of course, and it's tempting to send it all at once. But here's the thing – clients will assume that you rushed through it, or that you didn't take the time to do it properly."

Morgan crossed her arms. "I don't buy that."

He shrugged. "Happened to me with my first video, and Jackie actually gave me this same advice. She said to set those kinds of expectations and then exceed them – by a week, or two weeks. Whatever you can do. But *never* send your finished work right away."

"Really?" Morgan sat, studying him. "Jackie told you that?"

He nodded. "She did. She had some bad experiences with it herself."

"That's so weird."

"I know. But if you think about it, most people can't tell a good picture from a terrible one. So if you make them think it took a long time, they'll think it's better."

"That's manipulative," Morgan said.

He laughed. "I don't know about that, but I'm *telling* you, it's good business practice. Trust me. Or at least ask Jackie, and trust her."

She looked at him for a moment before pulling her phone out again. "Don't take this personally, but I'm going to ask her right now."

He put his hands up. "Go right ahead! I know that I need to earn your trust as a partner."

"Er – yeah." She put her phone away. "How far along are you with their video?"

"Oh, I'm done with it."

"Really?"

He crossed his arms and turned towards her. "You sound so surprised."

"I mean, you just seemed so...laid-back about it all."

"If you're asking me if I truly care about these people's weddings," Luke said with a shrug, "you're right. I don't care."

She laughed. "Okay, well then –"

He held up a hand. "However! I maintain that sometimes, I can do an even *better* job because I don't care."

"How is that supposed to work?"

"It keeps me from getting emotional. And I'm English, so I'm already not terribly emotional like you people are."

"*You* people?" Morgan replied in a high pitched voice.

"I'm not criticizing you, it's actually quite refreshing. A country full of passion!"

She scrunched her eyebrows. "Right."

"You'll see. Emotions can run high at times, and I'll be there to smooth it over."

The cars ahead of them started to move, and Morgan followed suit. "Well, I think we're going to be fine today. I got a chance to meet with this bride and she's one of the sweetest girls ever."

"The bride isn't always the problem, you know."

"I know! I'm just saying – I think it's going to be a really nice wedding. It's not very big, only fifty people, and the ceremony is being held on the top of Mount Constitution."

"Ah, that does sound lovely. Right, I will keep my opinions to myself."

Morgan rolled into her spot on the ferry and slowed to a halt. "Perfect!"

"Now how about we go upstairs and get a bite to eat?" said Luke.

"You don't have to ask me twice."

The ferry ride from Friday Harbor to Orcas Island was relatively short; they had just enough time to buy some food and eat while looking out over the water. Luke felt he did a decent job of not annoying Morgan for the duration of the trip – he mainly focused on asking her about her experiences as a photographer, the equipment she liked to use, and what her plans were for her business.

Perhaps later he'd be able to sneak in some more personal questions, but the camera talk got them all the way back to the car.

"Have you ever been to Orcas Island?" he asked as they prepared to depart.

"No. I've been to Lopez Island and Shaw, but I never had the chance last year to go to Orcas."

"Well this is quite exciting then!" Luke clapped his hands together. "The fun starts right off of the ferry terminal – we'll have to drive up a steep and winding road. Where are we meeting the bride again?"

"She's staying at a bed and breakfast in Eastsound. From there we'll go up the mountain for pictures."

"Excellent. Did you know that Mt. Constitution is the tallest point in all of the San Juan Islands?"

"I did not," Morgan replied as she drove the car carefully off of the ferry and back onto land.

"I am full of interesting – no, *fascinating* information."

Morgan laughed out loud and Luke felt a jolt of excitement. She couldn't completely dislike him if she laughed at his jokes, right?

"Then it's an honor to drive you around, sir."

They followed traffic and made good time getting to the bed and breakfast. Morgan called the bride, Allie, as she was parking to let her know that she was on her way up.

When they got to the room, Morgan introduced Luke as her second shooter. They seemed quite nice, but ten minutes in, a familiar face arrived. Ruby Edelsmith.

"And what's this?" Ruby said as she walked into the room, arms crossed.

"Hi there! I'm Morgan Allen, the photographer."

"That's fine," replied Ruby. "But what are you doing with *the dress*?"

"Oh! I was just getting some pictures for –"

"No one is supposed to see the dress. *No one*!"

Ruby snatched the gown in one swift motion and stormed away.

Morgan shot Luke a terrified look and he immediately felt the urge to jump into action.

"Don't worry – I'll handle this."

Morgan grabbed his arm to stop him. "No, don't. I don't know what I did –"

"You didn't do anything," said Luke. "She's just a –"

"Of course *you're* here," Ruby said when she returned.

Luke smiled and delicately took one of Ruby's hands to plant a kiss. "Ruby, my dear, it's so good to see you again. Have you met my new partner Morgan?"

"The one who was putting her dirty hands all over that pristine dress?"

Luke gently patted her hand, though he had the urge to drag her out of the room. "That's not what we were doing at all. We were simply following the bride's instructions."

"Well I've got news for you, Luke. I'm coordinating today and I'm not going to tolerate any shenanigans."

"I would never dream of it," said Luke.

He had to force himself not to smile – at the last wedding where he had to work with Ruby, he paid the flower girl five dollars to throw a large piece of wedding cake onto Ruby's dress. It got her out of the way for almost half an hour – well worth the money.

"And we already have a schedule laid out for the pictures," said Morgan, stepping forward with a printed sheet of paper clutched in her hand. "So I can just make sure that my schedule lines up with yours and –"

Ruby snatched the paper from Morgan. "No, no, no. Nope. *None* of these times work. We don't have time for makeup right now. I think it would be best if we got some of the pictures out of the way and you added in the makeup with the computer."

"I'm sorry but that's not possible," Morgan stammered. "And I'm not sure how that would even save any time because –"

Ruby sighed dramatically and rubbed her forehead with the palm of her hand. "I don't have time for a diva photographer. We're going to get some outdoor shots now before the hair and makeup girls arrive."

"Do you expect us to edit the dress onto her as well?" asked Luke.

"I don't care what you do," said Ruby as she glared at him. "Just make it work."

"Give me a second here with my partner," Luke said with a smile.

Ruby shrugged and left the room.

"What just happened," whispered Morgan. "Do you *know* that woman?"

"Unfortunately I do. Every once in a while, some poor, unsuspecting bride is subjected to crazy Ruby. I don't think that she's a real wedding coordinator – she's just a kooky lady that lives on the island. I imagine her house has a lot of wind chimes. Like a chorus of them, and a lot of home made bird feeders. Her house probably smells like moth balls and incense. Not the good stuff."

"What's the good stuff?" asked Morgan.

"Never mind – but really, I found that with Ruby, it's best to assert your dominance early."

"I don't want to upset the bride..." said Morgan, her voice trailing off.

"Don't worry, we won't."

Morgan bit her lip. Her face looked pale and her eyes were wide with fright. Luke felt something stir in his chest.

He took her by the hands. "Hey – it's going to be okay. Can you trust me, just this once?"

She hesitated just as Ruby's voice boomed over them, barking orders.

"I don't think I have a choice," Morgan said.

He smiled. "Perfect."

Luke made his way to Ruby, who was having a conversation with the bride, their faces only inches apart. He shuddered; the poor girl was getting heavy flow moth ball breath.

"I just want to make sure that we're on the same page," he said cheerfully. "Here is the schedule that we laid out for photos. What's your schedule, Ruby? I'd like to compare."

"Well – I don't have it all written out. I'm a pro, so –"

"Right. Allie dear, how about you take this pen and mark any areas where you'd like to make some adjustments – as per Ruby's schedule."

Allie looked between them, accepting the pen. "I think if we just...flip-flop these two things, we should be good?"

"Great!" said Luke, taking back the schedule. "Now Ruby dear, I'm going to give this to you. Make sure you don't lose it, okay?"

"But we need to –"

"Do what the bride wants, exactly. At the end of the day, that's what we're paid for, right?"

"But I really think that if we skip –"

"Good! We're on the same page. We're going to finish taking the pictures of the dress and the jewelry, I will go and visit the groom and make sure he's awake, and once the makeup girls get here, we can move onto step two. Be a doll and bring the dress back in?"

Ruby stared at him for a moment, clearly weighing her options.

"Alright," she finally said.

Luke turned back to Morgan, who was watching anxiously from the corner.

"See?" he said to her. "I'll have to repeat that process every hour for the next, oh, I don't know – twelve hours or so. Eventually she *does* fall asleep."

"What a nightmare," Morgan whispered, shifting the camera in her hands.

Luke shrugged. "Don't worry about it – we've got this."

For the first time since Ruby's appearance, Morgan smiled. "I never thought I'd say this, but I'm really glad that you came."

"I will take that backhanded compliment and cherish it forever," Luke said, accepting the dress from Ruby. "Now let's get back on schedule, eh?"

Chapter 9

That Monday, Matthew had the day off. He was still getting used to life on the island and asked Chief Hank for recommendations for what to do with his time.

"I don't know what you kids do. Bonfire on the beach? Take a girl to the movies? Look at cat pictures on the internet?"

"Uh, right – thanks," responded Matthew, sufficiently embarrassed.

The only girls he'd met on the island were through Chief. They seemed nice, but Morgan thoroughly interrogated him and Jade hardly said a word. They didn't give him the vibe that they'd want to hang out with him at a bonfire. Or share cat pictures.

Matthew had yet to make any friends on the island. Some of the deputies were friendly with him, sure, but they were all married with families. He felt silly asking them to go fishing or grab a beer – was he supposed to invite the deputy and the spouse? Or the kids too? How did that work?

And if he went by himself to go hiking or boating, he was afraid he'd look like a weirdo. In fact, if he went kayaking by himself he would probably never be seen again after being swept away by the sea.

So for his day off, Matthew decided to spend his time on something that mattered – the case of Kelly Allen. The intensity of Morgan's eyes stayed with him; he could sense how serious she was about her mother's case beneath her somewhat joking tone. He couldn't blame her – her mother was gone and she wasn't getting any answers. He requested that Chief let him take a look at the case.

It didn't take much convincing. Within twenty minutes, he dropped a pile of thick papers on his desk. "Here it is. And I'll email you a couple of things too. Maybe you can find something that we didn't."

"That's what I'm hoping," replied Matthew.

In an attempt to be social, he decided to look over the files at a coffee shop in town. He just had to keep an eye out for Morgan – Chief warned him that if she got ahold of the file, there was no telling what she would do. Apparently, she was a bit of a hothead.

Matthew chuckled to himself as he settled into a corner table at Oyster Coffee. There was definitely something that Chief wasn't telling him; obviously she'd gotten herself into trouble before. Matthew hoped that he'd get more invites to Sunday dinners – they were the only people that he knew outside of work and he enjoyed spending time with them. Maybe, if he was lucky, he'd get to hear how Morgan earned such a frightful reputation. Or he'd get to hear Jade say anything at all. She was rather mysterious.

He forced himself to focus and spent the next hour carefully reading over every aspect of the case. There were some surveillance videos that pieced together a bit of the timeline, and he watched each one carefully on his laptop. He was disappointed to find that each piece of evidence ultimately turned into a dead end.

Matthew was deep in thought, staring at a grainy picture of a woman driving a Corvette when a voice jarred him from his thoughts.

"Is this some sort of strange homework assignment?"

Matthew looked up and saw one of the employees of the coffee shop towering over him.

"I'm sorry, are you guys closing?" asked Matthew, noticing that the coffee shop was otherwise empty.

He shook his head and took a seat at the table. "No, nothing like that. We're still open for five more hours. I'm just horribly bored and couldn't help but notice that you seem to be doing something interesting."

"Oh, I guess you could say that." Matthew quickly shuffled some of the papers together to cover up the photographs. "It's a case that I'm working on."

"Oh that *is* interesting! Are you a detective?"

"No, not exactly," Matthew said, shaking his head. "I'm a new corporal at the sheriff's department."

"A copper! Nice to meet you, I'm Luke Pierce."

"Matthew Stevens, nice to meet you."

"Hang on, have you got a gun? And if so, can I...borrow it for a few minutes?"

Matthew laughed. "I do have a gun, but it's not on me right now. And I'm sorry, but no, you can't borrow it."

Luke snapped his fingers. "Too bad. I've never shot a gun, thought it might be fun. What's this case that you're working on?"

"I'm sure that you've heard of it – that woman who was killed on the island?"

Luke shrugged. "I've only been here a few months, and I'm quite sure I haven't heard of any murders."

"Oh, right, then this was before your time. She was the victim of a hit-and-run, and we still haven't caught the driver. Is there any chance that you guys might have some surveillance videos from about a year and a half ago?"

"Sorry, I wish I could help. But this building was completely empty up until a year ago. The owners fixed it up and turned it into a coffee shop."

Matthew frowned. "Alright, it was worth a shot. The case has gone cold and I'm trying to see if I can find anything that was missed."

"Dedication, I like it. How did you get into this line of work?" asked Luke.

Matthew was about to answer, but saw that there was a young woman standing at the counter, looking around for someone to help her. He motioned towards her.

Luke sighed. "Do you think if I just stay still that she'll go away?"

Matthew laughed. "What?"

The girl turned around and spotted them.

"There you are!" she said. "I was hoping I'd get to see you here, you're *never* here anymore, what's up with that?"

Luke smiled "What can I say? I'm in high demand."

"I bet you are," she said with a giggle.

Matthew, stuck between them, felt that the polite thing to do would be to excuse himself. He was about to say something when Luke spoke again.

"Listen, I'm on break, but I'm sure that Beth can help you with whatever you need?"

The smile faded from her face. "Oh. Okay. Well – my offer still stands. You know where the farm is!"

She walked off. Once she was safely out of earshot, Matthew leaned in and said in a hushed voice, "How did *you* get into this line of work? Seems like you keep things interesting."

Luke laughed. "I gave her a free drink *once*, and now she keeps asking me to go horseback riding with her."

"Not your type?"

"Horses? Definitely not. I prefer when I fully control the transportation – and when it doesn't bite."

Matthew laughed. "I meant her."

"Oh!" said Luke. "Eh – not really. How long have you been a cop?"

"Not long, actually," said Matthew. "Just over a year. I went to school to be an engineer."

"And that didn't work out?" Luke said, leaning in.

"Well – I had a job, if that's what you mean. And I wasn't terrible at it, I don't think."

Luke continued, apparently completely unaware that the girl was staring at him longingly. "So what made you change careers? And come here?"

Matthew shrugged. "I was – unsatisfied with my old life. My old job, the same thing day after day. Trying to pile up money for a big house I didn't want, or a truck I didn't need."

"Minimalist, I like it."

"One day I realized it was now or never, so I quit and started as a deputy back home in Oklahoma."

Luke frowned and crossed his arms. "That's one state that I haven't been to. This country is bloody enormous."

"It is," Matthew said. "My girlfriend at the time was pretty unhappy that I wanted to be a police officer."

"And that didn't change your mind?"

Matthew sighed. "No. Things were...complicated. We broke up. I took a promotion and moved here. Been here for a few weeks."

"That truly is fascinating," said Luke. "Meanwhile I've been hiding in this coffee shop trying to avoid horses."

They both laughed.

"Maybe I should become a cop," mused Luke. "Is it difficult?"

"Everything has its challenges."

"Have you gotten to shoot anything yet?"

"No, and hopefully I never have to."

Luke waved a hand. "Right, of course. What happens if you find the killer in this case?"

"The woman's family will be very happy. She left behind a husband and a daughter."

"Oh, that's much too serious," said Luke, standing up. "I imagined being a cop to be something like you see on TV, with high speed chases. Not mourning families."

Matthew laughed. "I'm sorry, there haven't been any high speed chases. Unless you count me chasing down geese."

"You've really ruined it for me," said Luke. "But anyway, welcome to the island. On Wednesdays we have an open mic night here – my roommates usually come to embarrass themselves. And on Fridays we do a trivia night."

"Here at the coffee shop?"

"No – there's a pub on Spring Street – we're looking for another team member."

Matthew wasn't particularly skilled at trivia, but it was something to do. "That sounds great! I'll be there."

Luke clapped his hands together. "Excellent. Friday at eight. And now I'm going to see if I can skip out on this shift early. Nice meeting you, Matthew."

"Nice meeting you too."

He watched as Luke left, another girl eyeing him. There was no way this guy was short on friends.

Matthew was glad that he decided to come to the coffee shop – as much as it would've been easier to sit at home in the dark, forcing himself to be social was actually a good thing. He wasn't good at making friends, so he was grateful that Luke was so talkative – even if he seemed preoccupied with borrowing his gun. He'd have to be careful about that.

Matthew reopened the folder in front of him. His next goal was to focus on the primary link in the case – Brock Hunter. Something told him that this could take a while.

Chapter 10

"That was incredible," Morgan said as she cleared the dishes from the table. "Where did you find that recipe?"

"Just at this website online. I think I overcooked the pork a bit," said Jade.

"No, absolutely not! It was perfect. And what was that on top?"

"Homemade nectarine salsa."

"I *loved* it!" Morgan gushed as she rinsed off the dishes. "I really need to step up my game here in roommate dinner making."

"Please don't worry about it," Jade said as she packed the leftovers into containers. "I know that you're really busy."

"I'm not busy. And I need to get better with cooking. Can you send me the website where you find all these recipes?"

"Sure!"

Morgan finished loading the dishwasher and felt her phone buzz in her pocket. She eagerly pulled it out – maybe she could find a few recipes and go grocery shopping to get the ingredients. But when she saw that it wasn't a message from Jade with the recipe website, she frowned.

Of course Jade noticed right away, because Jade noticed everything.

"What's that?"

Morgan stuffed the phone back into her pocket. "Nothing."

"Who was it? Did someone call you?"

Morgan shook her head. "Nothing, just work."

A smile spread across Jade's face. "By work do you mean that cute British guy?"

"I wouldn't call him cute," Morgan replied. "It would go right to his head, and his head is big enough already."

"Aw he's not so bad, is he? I thought he really helped you at this last wedding."

"He did, but..."

"But what? You don't like having someone around who's as pushy as you are?"

Morgan put her hands on her hips. "What's *that* supposed to mean!"

Jade laughed. "Just what I said. You like being in charge. And you're not used to...working with someone like you."

Morgan put up a hand. "No, no, *no*, we are *not* alike."

"If you say so. What did he want?"

Morgan debated telling Jade anything more. But who was she kidding – she knew that she was going to tell Jade everything. She didn't like hiding things or keeping things bottled up.

"He said that he got out of his shift at the coffee shop early, and wanted to stop by and show me some of the wedding videos he's put together."

"Inviting himself over?" Jade mused. "That sounds like something that you would do."

"*Stop*," groaned Morgan.

Jade settled onto the couch with a bowl of ice cream. "Oh come on, I'm just teasing. You tease me all the time."

"That's true," replied Morgan.

"So what? Are you going to let him come over or not?"

Morgan sighed. "I don't know – it seems weird."

"Why? Maybe he likes you."

"No," Morgan said flatly. "He definitely doesn't like me. I mean he's nice to me, but everywhere we go, women hit on him. It's ridiculous."

"But what if he only has eyes for you," Jade said in a whimsical tone.

"I don't think so."

"Okay fine. He at least wants to share his work with you, right? Don't you want to have a good relationship with him?"

"I mean, I guess." Morgan shrugged. "He's been really welcoming and introduced me to everyone that he knows in the business."

"See! He's trying to be a good partner."

"But he openly admits that he doesn't care about being a videographer!"

Jade took a bite of ice cream before responding. "You know people don't always mean what they say, right?"

"Yeah..."

Why was she even tempted to let him stop by? Luke was a total playboy. Women practically threw themselves at him, and it made her feel uncomfortable every time it happened.

At first she thought it might just be weddings in general that were like that – maybe people were inspired by the love that they saw, or driven mad by their own loneliness. She wondered if groomsmen or wedding guests would try flirting with her.

It never happened. Not once. Not even with a flirty grandpa.

Nothing!

Pathetically, she found herself hoping that one of the groomsmen at the last wedding would flirt with her. One of them seemed to be paying her a lot of attention from across the room when she was taking candids. He kept waving at her, then motioning at his face. She thought about winking at him, keeping it cute yet professional.

But it turned out that he was trying to tell her that she had icing on her cheek.

It was all silly. She didn't need men to hit on her; she wasn't there to flirt. And so what if Luke got hit on all the time? She didn't care. Luke wasn't even Morgan's type. She didn't know what her type was exactly – but definitely not some guy who thought he could have any girl he wanted. He couldn't have her!

"Earth to Morgan," Jade called out.

"Oh – sorry. Did you say something?"

"Yeah – I think you should invite him over. I'd like to see what kind of work he does."

"Well then why don't *you* invite him over!"

Jade giggled. "I would if I had his number."

"Okay fine – I'll tell him he can stop by."

"Great!"

Morgan sent the text to Luke and then went to her room. She felt like she needed to have something ready to show him. To her surprise, Jackie said that Luke's advice was correct – she really shouldn't send off all of the wedding pictures early, even if they were edited and ready to go. She was almost done working through the pictures from the wedding with Ruby – she could show those to Luke.

Ah, Ruby. What a wedding that was. As soon as she got home from it, Morgan told Jade all about the ridiculous things that Ruby tried to do. Inevitably, that's how Jade heard about how well Luke handled things.

It *was* impressive – Morgan couldn't begrudge him that. He seemed to actually enjoy it, which was odd to her. But

Morgan felt like she was finally starting to get her sea legs too – she was even able to redirect Ruby a few times towards the end of the night.

Truthfully, it took her a while to come out of her shell. She appreciated that Luke never said anything about how shy she could be. She hated herself for getting that way – she wasn't a shy person! It was just that she was trying so hard and wanted *so* badly to be liked and to do a good job.

It made her behave in strange ways. No wonder Luke did so well with brides and wedding coordinators and drunk guests. By his own admission, he just didn't care. What could be easier than not caring?

The doorbell rang. Morgan felt a little leap in her stomach. She didn't like that she felt that way and sternly told herself that Luke was *not* the right kind of guy for her, and that she needed to resist his charms, no matter what Jade said.

But he was still a valuable colleague, and as a professional, she needed to be able to maintain good relationships. She unplugged her laptop from her desk and carried it with her to the living room.

"Hey, how's it going?" Morgan said as she opened the door.

"Good, very good," he replied. "Oh shoot. I should have asked you if you wanted something from the coffee shop. I totally forgot."

"Oh no, that's okay. It's too late for me to have caffeine, I won't be able to sleep."

"Okay good. Next time I won't be so inconsiderate."

Next time?

She got out of the doorway so he could step inside.

"Hello Jade, nice to see you again!"

"Hi Luke," Jade stood and gave a quick little wave.

"It smells incredible in here," he commented. "Morgan, you didn't have to make dinner for me."

"Don't worry, I didn't," she said. "But Jade made dinner for *me* and it was amazing."

"Are you hungry? We have some leftovers," Jade said, walking towards the kitchen.

"No, but that's quite kind of you, thank you."

Jade continued. "And you know, we have a regular Sunday dinner at my mom's house on Westcott Bay. You should come out some time. She's a wonderful cook."

Morgan slowly turned to glare at Jade, but Jade refused to look at her. *Coward!* Why was she getting so pushy about Luke all of a sudden? Was she enjoying making her squirm? Was this pay back? Had she been planning this all along? What had gotten into her!

"That sounds delightful! I am busy this Sunday..."

Morgan waved a hand. "Don't worry about it, it's fine."

He smiled. "But I'm free next Sunday?"

"Oh, great!" Jade replied. "I think my future step-sister is coming into town that weekend. I could use some backup."

Morgan raised an eyebrow. Did Jade really want Luke around Amanda? That seemed like...a recipe for Amanda to yell at Luke.

"Oh, a step-sister? That sounds intriguing. I've got one of my own," Luke said. "I'd love to be your backup."

"Great! Well, I'll leave you two to your work. Nice seeing you again!"

"You too!"

Morgan watched as Jade disappeared into her room. She made a mental note to have a conversation with Jade later about *what on earth* that was about. Was Jade falling under his spell? She could have him then!

"Anyway," Luke said, turning to her, "I just wanted to pop over with my videos for some feedback."

"From me?" asked Morgan. "I mean – I'm happy to take a look, but I'm no expert."

"I value your opinion. May I –"

"Oh, yes, we can sit here." Morgan motioned to the couch.

They spent the next forty-five minutes watching and commenting on Luke's videos. Morgan was impressed – Luke had a distinct style that he brought to each video and the shots were beautiful. The editing was crisp, the music was timed perfectly and it seemed like he knew the footage quite well. She had little advice to offer.

"How are your pictures coming?" he asked once they were through.

"Not bad. I'm almost done with Saturday's pictures. And Jackie got back to me."

"And?"

Hm. He *did* have a nice smile. And always just a touch of dark stubble. Was that intentional – did he *know* that it made him more handsome? Or was it another side effect of his laziness, and he didn't like to shave?

"What did she say?" he prompted.

"That you were telling the truth," said Morgan, sitting back and crossing her arms.

"Oh ye of little faith. I always tell the truth."

What kind of person could say that so confidently? "Nobody *always* tells the truth."

"I do. People just don't take me seriously."

"I can't imagine why!" Morgan stood up from the couch. "What about when you lied to the bride about that sunset video?"

He frowned. "I maintain that I didn't lie. She just chose to assume what I meant."

"Uh huh. Can I get you something to drink? Or some ice cream?"

He leaned forward. "What sort of ice cream do you have?"

Morgan paused. "Oh wait. You probably don't eat ice cream."

"What do you mean? You think I'm a liar *and* I don't eat ice cream?"

"You're just all..." she waved a hand from the top of his head to his torso. "Fitness-y. You look like you're one of those people who doesn't eat carbs. Like you work out and...I dunno, don't eat ice cream."

He narrowed his eyes at her and a smile spread across his face. Morgan immediately regretted what she said, but it was too late.

Why did she let that come out of her mouth?

"Is that right?" He said, standing up. "If I didn't know any better, I'd say that you were checking me out."

"Oh my gosh, no, I wasn't. I just have never seen you eat – never mind. Do you want some or not?"

"Well now I feel like I *have to* have it to prove a point. I'm an ice cream eater, and a truth teller. And a gentleman. And a –"

"Okay Luke, I believe you." Morgan said as she opened the freezer.

He followed her into the kitchen. "What's that supposed to mean?"

"I don't know." She shrugged. "For one thing, as someone who doesn't care about being a videographer, those videos were pretty good."

"They're as good as they need to be. I like to be sure that I'll be paid for my work."

"It doesn't seem like you're inexperienced, either. Did you go to school for that?"

Luke shook his head. "Not exactly. I did make a lot of videos at university, but that was more for fun. My father was convinced that I was going to be a barrister like him."

"Oh, it's all making sense now." Morgan scooped three scoops of ice cream into her own bowl and offered Luke the spoon so he could serve himself. "Are those the lawyers that wear the wigs?"

Luke laughed. "Yes, those are the guys that wear the wigs."

"I can't imagine why you wouldn't want to do that."

"First off, it's a life sentence of horrible hat hair. I couldn't imagine why anyone would want that," said Luke. "Which is why I'm here."

She nodded. "Right. Trying to find yourself. Outside of your father's wig-wearing expectations."

He finished scooping his ice cream and shot her a look. "If that's what you want to believe, you can, but that's *not* what I'm doing. I don't think that life is as serious as you make it out to be. I do what I feel like doing. My father wanted me to follow in his footsteps, but I didn't. So I took all of the money that I had, flew to New Jersey, and bought a car."

"Interesting. And then you drove all the way here?"

"I did. There were many beautiful sights along the way, a few fantastic cities, some gorgeous national parks. I worked odd jobs here and there, as I needed to. And when I got to San Juan Island, I decided to stay for a bit to save up some money."

"And you just decided, on a whim, to be a videographer."

"Well," he leaned in, "not on a whim. It sort of just worked out."

Must be nice for things to just work out. "I see."

Morgan dropped her empty bowl into the sink. She probably shouldn't have eaten so quickly in front of him – but she wasn't thinking. She reminded herself that she didn't care if he thought she was lady like. "So in all this travel and trying to find yourself, you never told a lie?"

"Have I ever lied to you?"

Morgan shrugged. "Not that I know of."

"And I never will."

"It's interesting to me." Morgan crossed her arms. "You seem oblivious that you're lying to yourself."

Luke's jaw dropped in mock shock. "Well I never! Finding myself, lying to myself. You think you know everything about me."

Morgan smiled. She didn't feel like she knew Luke in the least. But in actively trying to resist his charms, she was able to focus on other things, like his motives.

"I don't know much about you," Morgan admitted. "But I know when a person is running from something."

"And how do you know that?" he said, a smile on his lips.

"Because I know that urge well. I know that fear, and the impulse to hide."

Luke leaned back, crossing his arms. "Now that can't be true. You don't seem like you've been afraid a day in your life."

"Yeah right!" Morgan laughed, but realized he was being serious. "That's funny you think that. I'm afraid all the time. I know fear well. I just...don't want to run."

Luke studied her for a moment. "Interesting."

Despite trying to resist it, Morgan yawned. She covered her mouth with her hand – no need for him to see directly down her throat while he was trying to figure her out.

"Oh gosh, I seem to have overstayed my welcome," he said. "I'm boring you to death."

Morgan shook her head. "No, you're not. It was actually really nice talking to you. And seeing your work."

"Oh goodness, don't call it my 'work,' that sounds too serious."

Morgan rolled her eyes.

"Right, well, I'm heading off, I guess I'll see you at that Sunday dinner."

Dang it Jade. He wasn't going to let that go. "Oh right, see you then!"

Morgan saw him to the door and watched as he got into his comically run-down car. For a moment she was afraid it wasn't going to start and she'd have to drive him home – but after two false starts, it started right up. Morgan waved – he waved back.

She closed the door and paused to lean against it. There was something about him – beneath the charm and the flirting and the great hair. There was actually a *lot* more to Luke Pierce, even if he refused to admit it. Morgan felt a bit sad that her next two weddings didn't include him – they seemed to make a good team after all. A good *professional* team.

Chapter 11

Of course his car wouldn't start – it gave her the chance to stand there in the doorway, staring at him. What was she doing? Was she thinking of more mean things to say about him?

When he first got into his car, he fumbled with the keys and didn't turn the ignition long enough. It was a relief when the engine finally started – and that's when she waved.

That was an oddly friendly thing to do for someone who insisted on ripping his life apart. He waved back and quickly put the car into reverse. What was normally a clunky sounding engine now sounded like a purr – this wonderful machine would get him home.

There was no way he could go to that dinner – she'd convince herself that she knew even more things about him. He just said he'd be there to be nice. Now he wasn't even sure if he could keep working with her. Maybe they should go back to not talking? She wasn't right about him – no, she was just... rude. He didn't need to deal with her calling him a liar.

Luke caught himself speeding a bit on the way and had to remind himself to relax his foot on the gas pedal. He kept flicking through the radio stations as he drove; none of the songs seemed quite right and finally in frustration he shut the radio off entirely.

"The next car I get will have working Bluetooth," he muttered.

He got home in record time and parked his car on the street. The lights were on in the house – his roommates must be home. He walked through the front door to find all three of them in the living room; one of them was playing a game on the Xbox and the other two were watching.

"Hey guys," Luke said as he walked in.

Brad and Steve grunted their hellos.

"There's some leftover pizza in the kitchen," said Larry.

"Oh, thanks. I'm fine though," responded Luke. His mind drifted back to the ice cream. It was quite a lovely flavor...

"Are you okay?" asked Larry. "You look weird."

Luke laughed. "You always think I look weird."

Steve chimed in. "Well that's because you *are* weird."

"Now Steven," Luke said sternly, "Are you still upset about those pork chops that you burned last night?"

"Or the panini that you burned today?" added Brad.

"Or was it the burned pop tart that forced us to throw the toaster away?" asked Larry.

Steve smiled and shook his head, but kept his eyes focused on the screen. "You guys just don't understand what I'm trying to achieve here."

"Burning the house down?" asked Luke.

"One of these days I'm going to be a top chef," said Steve.

They all laughed, but for the first time, Luke wondered if Steve was somewhat serious. He did seem to undertake overly ambitious recipes, and he ended up ruining them every time. Was Steve lying to himself about his skill level? Or was he a terrible cook trying to improve?

"Are we still on for open mic night tomorrow?" asked Brad.

"Oh – right. I'm not working at the coffee shop tomorrow, but we can still go."

Brad nodded his approval. "Excellent. I'm finally ready to debut my new song. Macy is going to love it."

"I'm sure she will. I'll see you guys later," Luke said, heading upstairs.

He got into his bedroom, closed the door behind him and let out a sigh. It was fun having roommates – they were great guys. But the routine was getting dull. They did the same things every week – open mic night, trivia night. They sat at the same bar, they talked to the same girls. Sometimes there were tourists who filtered in, and each guy tried his hand at flirting with them, too. Steve argued that Luke had an unfair advantage because of his accent.

"It doesn't even matter what you say! You just have to open your mouth and they fall in love with you."

That wasn't quite true – Luke liked to think that he put quite a bit of effort into his flirtations. But he loved to annoy Steve, so he went along with it. The idea of doing that for the rest of the week seemed impossible, though. He wondered if he should volunteer to take more shifts at the coffee shop. He didn't need the money exactly, but he appreciated the distraction.

Maybe it was time to develop some sort of a hobby? When he was younger, making videos was his hobby. Now that he made videos for work, it didn't seem quite as fun. But maybe he could make something fun?

No – that wouldn't do. He didn't feel like doing that at all. What was another hobby that he could pick up? Maybe he could learn how to fix his car. At least that would be useful.

But no, that didn't seem fun. It might be time to go back to Seattle and hang out with his friends there? Surely there were some concerts or something interesting that they could do. Then again, he had that small wedding to shoot on Lopez Island on Sunday. It would be a hassle to have to go out on Saturday and be back by Sunday morning.

Luke laid down on his bed with a groan. There *had* to be something that he could do with his time. He heard that his roommates really liked the show *Game of Thrones*. There were about a thousand episodes for him to catch up on, but he decided that now would be as good of a time as any to start. He settled into bed, watching three episodes in a row before deciding to go to sleep.

The next day he volunteered to take a shift at the coffee shop, but he wasn't needed. Instead he followed a whim and rented a bicycle from the shop next door – he'd been meaning to do it but was always too busy. The bike shop owner recommended that he take one that had a motor, for uphill climbs; he took the advice, but reasoned that it was highly unlikely he'd use it. He was in shape, after all. Even Morgan, who thought he was a liar, couldn't help but notice that he was in shape. What was a few miles around the island?

His bravado lasted all of one hour; normally he drove his car wherever he needed to go, and he'd never realized quite how hilly the island was. It was painfully apparent on a bicycle. Going uphill was grueling and going downhill was, at times, terrifying. The roads were winding and more than once he came much too close to a car for comfort.

He hoped to ride from Friday Harbor to Lime Kiln Park, but he chose the entirely wrong route. He turned around long before he made it to the park. It was much too stressful, though the constant fear of death certainly kept his mind occupied.

When he got back home, he showered and tried to take a nap, but felt too restless. Morgan kept floating into his mind. No matter what he did, he couldn't avoid the thought of her – and they were not thoughts he felt like examining right then.

Before long, his roommates came home and it was almost time for the open mic night. They sat around and made fun of each other for about forty-five minutes before leaving. They were always good for a laugh.

They got to the open mic night and all of the regulars were there, including most of the other groups they often ran into – the tour guides (kayak and bike), scientists from the research center, and counselors from the day camp. Everyone was roughly the same age and had the same goals – to have fun and relax.

Luke ordered a flat white and sat at a table with his roommates. He wasn't really listening to them – they were scheming a way to hit on the girls from the bike tour company. There were no new faces that evening, which was fine by him. Luke wasn't in the mood for making friends.

His roommates bemoaned the lack of new people, though. If, for example, Morgan happened to show up, they would've been thrilled. But ultimately, she probably would've scared them off with her overly critical commentary.

Plus, it would've really creeped Luke out if Morgan showed up at *his* open mic night. Not that she was creepy – it would just be...odd. He didn't know *what* it was about her. They had a nice time yesterday, until she made him feel all unsettled. Luke *despised* feeling unsettled. It was all going fine until she decided to call him a liar.

Yeah! That's what it was. She called him a liar.

Actually, first she admitted that she thought he was attractive, which for some reason meant withholding ice cream from him, and *then* she called him a liar. It was all very confusing.

Luke took honesty seriously – but how was Morgan supposed to know that? Sometimes the things he said were so on the nose that people assumed he had to be joking. That was always fun – when he was telling the honest truth and people thought he was messing around. And he'd just keep repeating himself until everyone moved on.

But why would Morgan say that? She was convinced that he was trying to find himself, and that was a funny theory of hers, but it was far too head-in-the-clouds to apply to him. From a young age, his father ingrained the idea that he had a duty and a purpose. He'd say things like, "Your purpose is what defines you in a family like ours."

"Funny that," Luke would say. "I thought that this family defined me by the piles and piles of money that I'd need to make to maintain the family honor."

His father hated it when Luke talked about money, even though it was the most important thing to him. "You don't have *anything* coming to you if you won't make something of yourself."

Luke didn't want money and he refused to follow his father's wishes. He had no need to find himself; he knew exactly who he was. He was the delinquent son of a barrister, a mediocre student and a disappointment. There were no longer any expectations on him. What more could he possibly be looking for?

"Don't screw this up, okay Luke?"

Luke turned to Brad, startled by the sudden mention of his name. "I'm sorry?"

Brad sighed dramatically. "Don't tell me that you weren't listening this entire time."

"I wasn't listening this entire time," replied Luke – truthfully.

Everyone except for Brad laughed. "Okay just listen – Macy's here. I'm going to perform my song right after her and it's going to *blow* her away. When she comes over here, you have to act like all of my music is as awesome as this one song."

Luke thought it was odd that Brad convinced himself that Macy would fall for him for the simple fact that one or all of his songs were "awesome," but he didn't want to rain on his parade.

"Done," Luke said with a nod.

Macy was the first to take the stage. Poor Brad was transfixed on her. Luke decided to be a good sport and pretend to listen, too.

Macy cleared her throat. "Hi everyone, tonight I'm going to share a poem I wrote – called 'Running from the Sunrise.' "

Luke could already feel his mind wandering. He looked at Brad, who was smiling and nodding while squinting his eyes.

Goodness it couldn't be *that* enjoyable? Luke made himself listen.

"I like to run in the mornings, and I like to run in the night. I like to run from the things that jump and bump and scare in the night."

Jump and bump and scare in the night? Was this woman running from a pack of raccoons digging in her trash bins? Surely it'd be more efficient to chase them off.

"I run when I am tired, I run when I am full. I run because it's the only thing that's keeping me from school."

Not only did she love running, she loved rhyming about running. Is this the kind of depth that Morgan thought he had? He wasn't running from anything! He was exploring a different country. He was looking for new adventures. Why did she think that he was running from something? What could he possibly have to run from? Everything back home was laid out for him – if he agreed to do as his father said, the path to becoming a barrister would be easy. It was terribly unfair; his competition didn't have a chance, despite being much more qualified.

But Luke had the family connection. The nepotism was disgusting. Luke wasn't running from that he was just...

He set his coffee down and rubbed his face in his hands.

"You okay man?" asked Larry.

"I *have* been running," said Luke finally.

"Shh!" said Brad, beginning to politely clap for the end of Macy's poem.

"I can't believe it," Luke muttered.

Brad was beaming. "I know, wasn't that great?"

Larry leaned in. "Did that really mess with your head, man?"

"It did!" Luke said, dropping his hands loudly on the table. "I mean, I'm not running from things that bump in the night."

"Stop it," warned Brad. "If you're here to make fun of people's art, you should leave."

Luke put his hand up. "No – I'm sorry, I'm not making fun. I sincerely feel the same way, just not – what I'm running from is my family's expectations."

"Just one more time, just to make sure," said Steve. "You're not in *any* way related to the royal family, right?"

Luke shook his head. "Not that I know of."

"Okay, just needed to know what we're working with here."

Macy appeared at the edge of the table. "Hey guys!"

"Evening," said Luke.

"Macy," Brad said, "that was *amazing*. I mean just the delivery, the words and stuff..."

Words and stuff? Luke gave him a side eye, but Macy didn't seem to notice. Her focus was on someone else.

"What did you think Luke?"

"It really made me think," he said.

"Wow, thanks," she said, her cheeks turning slightly red. "You know...I've been meaning to ask you if I could show you around the island. I've got free bike rentals – anytime you want."

He stared at her for a moment before it sunk in. "Oh. Oh!"

Normally he would relish the opportunity to torture one of his roommates by going out with a woman that they liked – and Macy was beautiful, despite her terrible poetry skills. But he couldn't be so cruel to Brad.

And her poem – though simple – just happened to be something that he needed to hear. Yet somehow, he doubted that Macy could be as insightful into his psyche as a certain photographer already was.

"That's very kind of you, but I'm afraid my schedule is booked. Brad loves bikes though."

A broad smile spread across Brad's face. "Oh yeah, I've got a great road bike. I bike everywhere."

"That's great!" Macy said. "Well I think you're up – good luck!"

They watched her walk away and return to her friends. Luke clapped a hand on Brad's shoulder. "Sorry, I tried."

He shook his head. "It's fine – I don't care. You can go out with her, I don't care."

"Come on Brad," said Luke. "She hasn't even heard your song yet!"

"Yeah," added Steve. "That's when things are really going to turn around for you."

Everyone, including Brad, erupted into laughter.

"It's tough," said Luke. "The ones we are in love with never seem to love us back."

"Yeah right man," Brad said as he stood up to go towards the stage. "Every woman on this island is in love with you."

Luke frowned. "Not every woman."

Chapter 12

They only had about ten minutes to finish getting ready before they would be late.

"Morgan," Jade called out from the kitchen. "Did you decide on an outfit yet?"

Morgan came down the hall in a huff. "I wasn't stressing out about my outfit, I just couldn't decide if I was going to be cold or not."

Jade smiled as she pulled the dessert she'd made out of the fridge. This was the first time that she felt ready to share her cooking with someone other than Morgan. Morgan made it easy – she ate anything that was placed in front of her and thought everything was delicious. Never once did she complain or suggest any changes.

But tonight there were other guests; Chief Hank was bringing his kids Amanda and Jacob to dinner. And as expected, Luke said that he wouldn't miss out on his invitation for the world.

"Are you sure that it has nothing to do with a certain handsome Englishman that's coming to dinner?" asked Jade.

Morgan groaned. "I can't believe you actually invited him."

"What?" Jade shrugged. "He seems like an interesting person. And you have to be friends, because you're working together a lot."

"That's true," said Morgan. "I think I might've offended him the last time we hung out though."

Jade stopped and turned towards Morgan. "What did you say?"

"I mean...you know how I just say things."

"Oh I know," Jade said. "What exactly did you say? How bad was it?"

Morgan shifted her weight. "He kept going on and on about how honest he was and I got really annoyed..."

"And? Did you get a microphone and read him the riot act?"

Morgan laughed. "No, that was a one time deal. But I did tell him that he's not completely truthful."

"Oh. That's an odd thing to say."

She crossed her arms. "Okay, what I said was that he's lying to himself."

"Morgan! That's kind of a serious thing to say to a colleague." But not to someone who was more than that...

"I know," said Morgan, placing a hand over her eyes. "He just pushes my buttons. Even if it wasn't the nicest, it was the truth."

Jade handed Morgan the dessert. "Can you carry this?"

"Sure. Mm that smells great – what is that?"

"Thanks! It's a lime mousse torte. And just – I mean this in the nicest way – maybe tonight you can practice stopping yourself before you say something you'll regret?"

"I feel like I shouldn't go," Morgan said. "I'm definitely going to say something inappropriate."

"You're an adult. You can do this. How about when I kick you under the table, you actually pay attention to me?"

Morgan took a deep breath. "Okay. That's actually not a bad idea."

"Good. Ready?"

"Ready!"

Despite Morgan's difficulty in getting dressed, they still managed to be three minutes early for Sunday dinner. The front door was unlocked and they let themselves in.

"Hey Mom!" Jade called out. "Is there room for the dessert in the fridge?"

"Hi sweetie! Yes, come on in."

"Should I set the table?" asked Morgan.

"No," her mom shook her head. "Everything is all set!"

Morgan put her hands on her hips. "Well there is some serious stuff going on here – what's on the menu for tonight Margie?"

"I wanted to make something that Hank told me his kids love. So for Amanda I made these crab cakes," she handed the dish off to Morgan. "And for Jacob, I did a Spanish rice bake."

Jade peered over at the Dutch oven filled with rice and chorizo. It smelled heavenly.

"And I have a pasta salad – spinach and feta pasta!" Her mom pulled a large bowl out of the fridge, removing the plastic wrap on top.

"They're going to love it Mom," Jade said with a smile.

They set the dishes on the dining room table just as there was a knock at the door.

"I'll get it," said Jade.

She was hoping that it was Chief Hank and his kids – Jade really wanted to make a good impression on them and it needed to start from the first hello.

Jade opened the door to find Luke standing there. "Hi Luke, so glad that you could make it. Come on in."

"Thanks so much for having me," Luke said as he stepped inside. "I wasn't sure what kind of party this was, so I've brought a red wine from France, my favorite Scottish ale, and a bottle of Mexican tequila."

A laugh escaped from Jade and she covered her mouth with her hand. "That's quite the world tour of alcohol."

He shrugged. "You never know when it might come in handy."

Her mom walked into the room, pulling off her apron. "Hi! Luke, is it?"

"Yes," he said with a nod. "You have a great memory Mrs. Clifton."

"Oh please," she stood on her tiptoes to give him a hug. "Call me Margie."

"Mom, Luke brought some red wine. And beer. And a *large* bottle of tequila."

"Oh my," said Margie. "Thank you so much!"

"I'm not sure that he was planning on sharing," said Morgan.

"I wasn't actually, so this is a bit awkward," replied Luke.

Everyone except for her mom took their seats at the table.

"This is the most impressive dinner I've ever seen," Luke said.

Morgan sighed. "Thanks, I did it all myself."

"Really?"

Morgan nodded solemnly. "Yes. I picked out this tablecloth last year when I was living in Margie's house."

"Oh, so you *didn't* make the food?"

"No, what gave you that idea?"

Luke shrugged. "It must be that *other* bottle of tequila that I had before I got here messing with my head."

Jade smiled – Morgan couldn't help but say what popped into her head sometimes. But Luke certainly didn't seem to mind.

"Hello!" called out a voice.

Jade's heart leapt. It was Chief Hank. She popped up from her chair, eager to say hello.

"Welcome!" Jade said, giving him a hug.

"Hey Jade, good to see you. This is my son Jacob, and this is my daughter Amanda."

Jade felt like her cheeks would crack from smiling. She offered a handshake to Jacob first, then to Amanda. "It's so nice to finally meet you both."

"It's really nice to meet you too – and this house is gorgeous!" said Jacob.

Amanda nodded and offered a small smile.

Morgan waved and introduced herself from her seat. Luke stood up to shake Chief Hank's hand.

"So you're the future evil stepfather?" Luke said.

Chief Hank laughed. "You don't hear a lot of stories about evil stepfathers, do you?"

"No," said Amanda coolly. "It's always the evil stepmother."

Jade felt like a rock landed in her stomach.

"That's right," Luke said as he returned to his seat. "However, I don't see how anyone could consider Margie to be evil. She strikes me as more of a fairy godmother type of character."

"Maybe Margie will be my fairy godmother," Morgan mused.

"Well if you lived in her house, wasn't she already a sort of fairy godmother?" asked Luke.

Morgan frowned. "That's a good point."

Jade's mother returned to the living room, a smile plastered on her face. "Hi everyone! Welcome, welcome! Please take a seat."

There was an awkward moment where they went to sit down, but then Chief Hank decided to introduce them. "Amanda, Jacob – this is Margie."

Jade could see that her mom was really holding back from hugging them both. "It's so nice to finally meet you – officially," she said.

"It's very nice to meet you too," said Jacob.

"Yes," Amanda said as she took a seat.

Jade returned to her seat as well, slightly more nauseous than when she got up. Maybe she just needed to eat something? They started passing around the plates right away, the group pleasantly entrenched in the chatter of travel. Jacob told them about his harrowing journey from Australia and how he was delayed for twelve hours in Los Angeles

"Now *there* is a city that I need to visit," said Luke. "Talk about an American icon."

"I wouldn't know," replied Jacob with a laugh. "But the airport was nice."

"How was your flight Amanda?" asked Jade.

She shrugged. "I didn't have any connections, so it was ten hours nonstop. That's pretty grueling itself."

"Oh yeah, definitely."

Jade didn't know why she was agreeing – she'd never been on such a long flight in her life. The longest trip she'd ever been on was to New York City to visit her dad. That wasn't too bad – she quite enjoyed the trip. It is very peaceful to be able to read or listen to music. Come to think of it, Brandon never wanted to go on trips, so she really was at peace during those times. No wonder she liked flying.

"Well Margie," Luke said, "I can confidently say that you are far over qualified to be a wedding caterer. Everything here is delicious."

"I thought you were a wedding planner?" asked Amanda.

Her mom shook her head. "I'm not either, actually. I just like to cook for fun. And I rent out the barn here on my property as an events venue. We do a lot of weddings. I can give you a tour after we're done!"

"So you're not a caterer," Amanda said, neatly folding her napkin on the table. "That's good."

That sick feeling hit Jade again. She looked at Amanda's plate – she hadn't taken very much food to begin with, and most of it sat there untouched. It almost looked like a strange piece of art, the vast empty spaces between food speaking volumes.

"Amanda," Chief Hank said in a low voice.

She sighed and threw her hair out of her face. "Yes Dad?"

He stared at her but said nothing.

"This was really lovely, thank you Margie," said Jacob. "Is it okay if I call you that?"

"Of course! You can call me whatever you like!"

"Well I wouldn't call you a good cook," Amanda said under her breath, but loud enough that everyone heard her.

The table was engulfed by silence. Jade felt truly sick, like she couldn't take another bite. She was afraid to look up.

A loud clang rang out as Morgan tossed her fork onto her plate.

Chapter 13

Everyone's eyes were on her. She needed to come up with something – and fast.

"Did you guys ever hear about the time that I crashed a party at the barn?" Morgan said, her volume a bit too loud.

Chief sighed. "Morgan, I don't –"

"No, no," she said, cutting him off. "It's a good one. I mean, it's definitely an embarrassing story about me getting all whipped up and being manipulated by Jade's ex-husband, but really, it was all me, embarrassing *myself*. At the *same* time, it was extremely funny, looking back. I feel like we all laugh about it now."

Jacob cleared his throat. "You just crashed a random party?"

"Well, no – it's kind of a long story," said Morgan, her mind spinning with how to put it all together. "I don't know if you know this, but Margie's ex-husband is my biological father."

"My, my," a smile spread across Luke's face. "This *is* quite a story. We're up to two ex-husbands."

She ignored him. "I didn't know it at the time when I met Margie, or when she invited me to live with her. So it's not like I was *planning* to ruin this party. And I was going through some pretty dark stuff – Chief, you remember."

He nodded but said nothing, arms firmly crossed against his chest.

"Well anyway," Morgan gulped down some water. "Margie was throwing a surprise birthday party for him. Here – at the barn. And she just found out that he was my dad. And I didn't know that he was my dad, or that my dad was even alive, until Brandon told me."

"Who's Brandon?" asked Amanda.

Good – she was getting involved. "Oh, he's Jade's ex-husband. He's...a real peach."

"Still working on divorcing him, actually," interjected Jade, lightly touching her forehead with her fingers.

"Sorry Jade – sensitive topic." Morgan outstretched her hand and patted her on the shoulder.

Jade smiled and waved a hand. "No, totally fine. We broke up because of this."

"Really?" asked Margie. "I don't think I knew that."

Morgan didn't want them going on a Brandon tangent, so she continued. "Right, so you're getting rid of him, which is great. Apparently, when he found out that I was related, he thought that I was going to try to go after Jade's inheritance or something. He told me that everyone knew that Jade's dad was *my* dad and they were all hiding it from me. This is getting confusing, but basically he got me all riled up."

"Which isn't hard to do," Jade said with a smile.

"Exactly," Morgan said to some laughter around the table. "And I snuck into this party right when they're doing speeches. Jeff – my biological dad – had the microphone. So I saw an opportunity, and I took it."

"The opportunity, or the microphone?" asked Luke.

"Both," Morgan said with a nod.

Jacob leaned forward, a puzzled look on his face. "Wait – is this a real story?"

"As real as they come," Morgan replied. Everyone laughed again. She was starting to feel pretty good about this. "So I grab the microphone, and I didn't want to have it taken away so I jumped on top of a table. I gave this *really* mean speech, and I said all kinds of mean stuff about my biological dad, and Margie, and a little bit about Jade too – sorry guys."

Jade was laughing now. "It's totally okay."

Morgan continued. "And of course, I say some mean stuff about Brandon, because he deserved it..."

"It doesn't seem you were terribly discerning about who did and didn't deserve it," Luke observed.

Morgan laughed. "Yeah, it was pretty bad."

"I can't believe that I missed this," Luke said, covering his mouth with his hand. "If I could invent a time machine, I would go directly to this moment."

Morgan turned to him. "Really? You don't want to see like FDR speak? Or – whatever, Churchill?"

"Who needs Churchill when you're insulting an entire family at their own surprise party."

"Well don't worry, I'm sure this is not the last stupid thing that I'll ever do."

Laughter made its way around the table and Morgan let out a sigh. It seemed she was successful in diverting the mood from taking a complete nosedive. Jacob picked up by telling a story about one of his roommates in Australia "who's a hothead, too."

Morgan thought of taking offense to that term, but she let it slide. The story didn't put her in the best light. She took a sip of wine and allowed herself a few more bites of food.

She knew that Amanda was looking for a fight, because she had employed that tactic in the past many times. The biggest difference was that Morgan wasn't as passive-aggressive as

Amanda. Actually, Morgan was generally just straight up aggressive.

Margie and Hank insisted on clearing the table once everyone was done, and Morgan and Jade fetched plates for dessert. Morgan knew that Jade was afraid of sharing her lime pie – or torte, whatever it was – with the group. Though Margie could handle a nasty comment, Morgan wasn't sure that Jade could. If Amanda decided to say anything mean about this dessert, Morgan knew she'd have to get back up on the table and start spitting insults.

Luckily, Amanda made no further comments. She was mostly quiet for the rest of the night, which wasn't ideal, but better than her trying to ruin the evening. Jacob behaved normally, and even Hank recovered. But whenever Morgan stole a glance at Margie, she could tell something wasn't right. Margie wasn't her normal bubbly self – she was still nice of course, but her cheeks were slightly pink the entire night and she didn't say much.

When she was done with her dessert, Amanda announced that she was still feeling jet lagged and wanted to go home. Jacob was agreeable to leaving, so Hank said goodbye – giving Margie a brief kiss on the cheek before going.

Luke was the first to speak after they left. "Well that was –"

"Don't!" warned Morgan.

He pulled away, a puzzled look on his face. "What? I was going to say that was a really nice dinner."

"Oh. Yeah Margie – it was very nice."

Margie offered a weak smile. "Thank you."

"Minus the one snafu, I'd say it was a successful meeting of the families," said Luke. "In my family, if no blood is spilled at dinner, we consider it a raging success."

Jade and Margie exchanged looks but said nothing.

Morgan sighed. "Somehow I feel like time has not helped Amanda."

"I don't understand why she's being such a brat," said Jade.

"Jade!" Margie exclaimed. "You shouldn't say things like that."

"Why not? She didn't even try to be nice. And then she said –"

Margie put up a hand. "I don't blame her, honey."

"Well I do!" said Jade. "I can't believe she was being so rude to you."

Morgan felt a twinge in her chest. Jade was a completely docile person except for two instances – when she was awoken before sunrise, and when someone she loved was hurt.

Margie let out a sigh and sat down at the table. "Hank said that she's having a hard time with our relationship."

"I don't see how it's her business," snapped Jade.

Morgan cleared her throat. "I don't agree with the way she's behaving...but I can't say that I don't understand."

Jade's eyes widened. "Are you serious?"

"Don't get upset. I'm just saying – I lost my mom recently too. And it's still a very raw thing and..." Morgan felt her voice start to break. Crap. She thought she might be able to talk about her mom without crying. Wrong.

"That's different," Jade said.

Morgan cleared her throat. "I know it's been longer for Amanda. But I don't know how I'd react if my dad was dating someone. Even if it was someone as wonderful as your mom. It would be tough. I wouldn't want to feel like my mom was...I don't know, being replaced?"

"I can't believe this!" Jade crossed her arms.

"It's very sweet of you to defend me," said Margie. "But Morgan's right. I think Amanda is struggling. I think she's still hurting very much."

"Well I hope that she can at least be civil towards you for the rest of this visit," said Jade. "I should get going, I have a really early day tomorrow and have to catch the ferry in the morning. Ready to go Morgan?"

"Oh, uh," Morgan stammered. "Right now?"

"I can drive you home," said Luke.

Morgan almost forgot that he was there. How awkward he must feel in this conversation. "Are you sure? I just wanted to stay and help clean up a bit."

"What a coincidence, I wanted to help clean up a bit too!"

Morgan turned to Jade and hugged her. "Please don't be mad at me. I don't want to fight."

"I'm not mad at you!" said Jade. "I promise."

"Good. I'll see you tomorrow then?"

Jade nodded. "Goodnight Mom."

"Goodnight sweetie."

Jade left and they quietly cleared the table. Morgan loaded the dishwasher as Margie packed up leftovers.

"I'm sorry to hear about your mother, Morgan," Luke said as he carried in a stack of dishes.

"Thank you." Morgan made sure not to look up from the plate she was rinsing. No need to get into this with Luke. "Margie – you're not going to be able to eat all of these left-overs by yourself, are you?"

"Oh, would you kids like to take some of these home?" she replied.

"I mean...if you're offering!" Morgan said with a smile.

"You don't have to take them just to make me feel better," said Margie. "I know it wasn't my best meal."

"Margie – it was delicious! Amanda was just in a sour mood. She'll get over it."

"Excellent work with that rambling story, by the way," said Luke. "I'm going to need a more in-depth history of all that."

"Thanks." Morgan laughed. "Maybe some other time."

Margie frowned. "I don't know if Amanda is going to get over it. I don't want her to think that I'm trying to replace her mom – in *any* way."

"Oh come on – she's just being moody. You can't let her get to you."

"I also can't marry her father and damage their relationship."

"Margie! Come on – it's not going to damage their relationship. You can't break up with Chief! You're an island power couple!"

She smiled. "I love him and I'll do what's best for him."

Morgan frowned. Why did that sound so ominous? How could Margie even think of breaking it off with Chief? Just because Amanda was being a little snotty?

"Luke – you saw how great they are together. Talk her out of this."

He put his hands up. "I'm not one to support weddings."

"Thanks for the help," she said, glaring at him.

Margie packed up the leftovers into two bags. "Don't worry about me Morgan. And thank you both so much for helping to clean up."

Morgan accepted both of the bags, handing one off to Luke. "No, thank *you* for having us. Don't do anything crazy, okay?"

"Yes," said Luke, "don't do anything that Morgan would do."

Margie smiled. "Have a good night. It was very nice seeing you again Luke."

"It was lovely, thank you for having me."

They got outside to Luke's car and Morgan groaned.

"What's the matter, did you forget something?" he asked.

"No. I just keep forgetting how much your car stinks."

"Dagger to my heart." He slapped a hand to his chest. It made an impressive thud. He definitely spent more time working out than he did eating ice cream. Morgan stood by her initial assessment.

"I'm just kidding. Thanks for the ride."

"Anytime." He ran to the passenger side to open the door for her.

Morgan eyed him suspiciously as she sat down. "Thanks?"

"I know that you're probably not used to a gentleman like me," he said, gingerly taking the seat belt and stretching it over her. "But I *insist* on taking care of my passengers."

Morgan couldn't help but laugh – he was so ridiculous. He buckled her in as she shook her head. He had a nice cologne – she'd never gotten close enough to smell it before. It smelled expensive.

He ran around the other side of the car and got into the driver's seat. "Are you sure you don't want any ice cream or late night coffee or anything before you go home?"

She shook her head. "I'm good, but thanks."

"Oh, alright." He started the car. "What about some other time this week, then? I was thinking that we never really get to spend quality time together while we're working. For example,

I never heard this wild story of you ruining your father's birthday."

"You never asked."

"You're right, but I didn't have a chance. Would you like to go to dinner with me? On Friday maybe?"

Oh dear. She hadn't expected that. Was he asking her on a date? Did he run out of gorgeous hiking magazine women to ask out? Maybe that was more of a Saturday type of date. Being a Friday date wasn't *too* bad, and at least he was giving her some notice.

He cleared his throat. "Or maybe something else – kayaking perhaps? I hear it's lovely, but I've been too terrified to try it."

"Oh yeah – I really want to try it too."

"I could get us a great deal on kayak rentals! Or on bicycle rentals. Actually – maybe not that. That might be too soon."

She scrunched her forehead. "It's too soon to go bike riding?"

He waved a hand. "Yeah, it's a long story. But kayaking? And then dinner?"

They really shouldn't be mixing their business lives with their personal lives. People always said that was a bad idea. "Oh – I don't know."

"Is it because we work together?"

She stole a glance at him – he appeared to be serious. "I mean – that's part of it."

"Okay. What's the other part? Have I offended you in some way?"

She laughed. "I mean – I don't know why you're being so insistent about this."

"Ah, you see it's very simple – I quite like you."

Morgan felt a jolt in her stomach. "Well that's pretty forward, don't you think?"

He shot her mischievous smile. "Oh please – you're one of the most forward people that I know. I thought you would appreciate that."

"How do I know that you're not just trying to..."

"Trying to what?"

Morgan laughed. She couldn't believe she was saying this out loud. "Trying to play me! You're kind of a big flirt and I'm not really –"

"Okay, it's true that I'm a bit of a flirt. But – my goodness, you're really making me say this aren't you?"

Morgan laughed. "I'm not making you do anything!"

He continued. "Alright. You must understand how difficult this is for an Englishman. But okay, here goes – I really, genuinely like you. I love spending time with you, and I want to get to know you better. And before you called me a liar –"

She groaned. "Are you ever going to forget that?"

"No – you were right. I was lying to myself. I can tell you all about it if you agree to go out with me!"

Morgan laughed. She couldn't believe that she was succumbing to his charms. It did seem like he was telling the truth, though. What was the worst that could happen?

Well – they could entirely ruin their professional relationship and she'd end up with a broken heart. That was all.

"Alright. Fine."

"Really? We're on, then?"

She turned to him and smiled. "Yes. Friday?"

"Friday! Good. I'll make a kayak tour reservation. Where would you like to eat?"

"Let's get pizza," she replied.

He smiled. "Somehow I knew you weren't going to say 'I don't care.' "

Morgan shrugged. "That's not really my style."

They arrived at her place and she decided to hop out of the car before she agreed to anything else. "Well – thanks again for the ride. And have a good night."

"You too."

She gently closed the car door and pulled out the keys to her house. For some reason, she felt a bit like she was walking on a cloud.

Chapter 14

It was too late that night when he got home to plan his date with Morgan, but first thing the next morning, Luke booked a kayak tour for two. He called the tour company where a friend of his worked – he wanted to make sure that they had a competent tour guide. He also wanted to make sure that the guide was male; there was no need to further stoke Morgan's suspicions about him being a flirt.

Okay, maybe he'd been a bit of a flirt in the past and hadn't taken dating seriously. Why would he, though? He initially planned to stay on San Juan for three months, tops, so he was never looking for anything serious. One thing led to another though, and he was still here.

And now...well, he didn't want to get ahead of himself, but after getting to know Morgan, his plans for leaving the island seemed less and less important.

For their date, he also tried to make a reservation at the best pizza place in town, but oddly, they didn't take reservations. How was he supposed to make this date perfect when Morgan chose cuisine that only had casual dining? He was glad that she was so decisive, though. Most girls tried to be overly agreeable and then didn't offer any suggestions.

After Luke was satisfied that he planned all that he could, he went for a five mile run near the Cattle Point Lighthouse. Morgan was always talking about how breathtaking it was, and he agreed. It was a beautiful place to take in the magnificence of the island. Despite what Morgan suggested, he didn't strictly use the rugged and rocky coasts to record sunrises and trick his clients. He enjoyed the views in *addition* to tricking his clients.

After his run, he took a shower and headed into Friday Harbor. One of the clients they were working with in a few weeks reached out to him and asked for a meeting. Her name was Jill – or Jillian, or something. Jackie did their engagement pictures a few months back, and now the bride was thinking of doing a pre-wedding interview as part of their video package.

Luke normally didn't suggest these to his clients because he found them annoying, but making one was easy enough. All he had to do was sit down with the bride and groom separately and ask them a preset list of questions. Then he would edit it all together with a whimsical flair and make it seem like their love was destined to be.

The bride's email was a bit intense, but it seemed like something that Morgan would do to make the client happy, so he decided to meet with the woman and be a professional. She was on the island that day for some wedding related activities, so he suggested meeting up at the coffee shop. He arrived promptly at noon and she was already there waiting for him.

"Hi there, nice to meet you, I'm Luke."

"I know," she said as she enthusiastically shook his hand. "I'm Jillian Rivers."

Luke paused for a moment – did they know each other? Was he supposed to recognize her? He studied her for a moment. She looked vaguely familiar, but Luke wondered if it was only because she had the standard sorority girl look – long blonde hair, heavy makeup and fake eyelashes. It was more her look that he recognized, though, and not so much the woman herself.

"I'm sorry, have we met before? How rude of me –"

She shook her head. "Kind of, and I'm a *huge* fan."

"Oh, thank you."

"And I was actually in a wedding a few months ago where you did the video, but I'm sure you don't remember me. I looked really different – I had this *horrible* teal dress and I weighed about twenty pounds more."

"Ah. I always say," he sat down in the chair across from her, "the more horrible the bridesmaids' dresses, then the more sincere the bridesmaids' love for the bride."

She laughed. "You're so right."

"Can I get you something? Coffee, tea?"

"Oh, what are you getting?"

"I'm partial to the cappuccino here," he replied. "You can add a caramel syrup to make it *really* something."

She smiled. "I'll have one of those!"

He reminded himself to smile. At least she was agreeable. "Hey Marcus! Can we get two caramel cappuccinos please?"

Marcus nodded. "Coming right up!"

"You just know everyone around here, don't you?" Jillian said, a smile fixed on her face.

"Not everyone. Well, maybe in this coffee shop. Anyway. I brought my laptop so I can show you some examples of pre-wedding interviews that I've done before. Do you want to take a look at them first or tell me what you had in mind?"

"I would love to see them," she said, leaning forward.

"Alright." He pulled his laptop from his bag and placed it on the table between them. "First up I have one that I did about two months ago. It's on the shorter side, but the bride was really interested in having something easy to watch for her friends and family."

"That sounds great."

Luke hit play and they watched as the bride and groom gushed about each other. Luke actually quite liked this couple – they were both sweet and genuine. He didn't even mind making the pre-wedding video for them. Actually, that was probably why it was so good – it had more to do with the couple than it had to do with him.

As the video came to an end, Luke reached forward so he could pause the video. But as soon as he had his hand on the computer, Jillian reached forward and placed her hand on top of his.

"It's surprising that you can do such artistic work with these strong hands."

Luke froze. His brain couldn't process what was happening. He'd spent plenty of time flirting with bridesmaids, of course, but *never* the bride!

The bride was normally focused and stressed out. The bride was usually running the show. And the bride was *always* off limits! If he could get her to laugh he considered it a win, but even *he* wouldn't sink so low as to hit on the bride at her own wedding!

"Oh – I didn't expect to see you here today," said a voice behind him.

Luke pulled away from Jillian's surprisingly firm grip and turned to see Morgan standing behind him.

Of course.

Her lips were pressed into a firm pale line.

"Morgan, I'm so glad you're here! This is Jillian Waters, we're shooting her wedding next month."

"Nice to meet you," Jillian said in a high-pitched voice. "And it's actually Ri–"

"Jill, this is Morgan, my partner. If you don't mind, I'm going to have a word with her."

"No problem, I'll just sit here and enjoy this *delicious* cappuccino."

He cringed at her saying the word "delicious" before following Morgan outside.

"It's not what you think," he said immediately. "She asked me to do a pre-wedding interview video for her, and –"

"Right, and you decided that you would have a little fling with our client, the bride-to-be."

Morgan stood with her arms crossed over her chest.

"No, I swear – she came on to *me*. She grabbed my hand and said something about me having strong hands, and I don't even have strong hands!"

Morgan let out a sigh before she responded. "What you do is your own business, Luke, but I wish you wouldn't involve our clients. It's going to be hard to shoot a wedding if you break the couple up beforehand."

"I'm not trying to have a fling with the bride!" Luke said. "You *have* to believe me."

"No actually, I don't have to do anything."

And with that, Morgan turned and walked to her car.

Luke groaned. He wanted to run after her, but he still had to deal with Jillian. He turned around to see Jillian's face in the window. She waved.

He turned back around and Morgan was already gone. Luke remained standing for a moment, forcing himself not to yell or throw a fit in front of the coffee shop. How did he even get into this situation?

Alright – this meeting from hell with Jillian needed to wrap up first, and then he could explain what happened to Morgan. He let out a deep breath and walked back to the coffee shop.

Chapter 15

She was halfway home when she remembered that her plan was to stop at the grocery store before going home; Morgan promised Jade that she would grab a few things for the house and for a recipe that they wanted to try. She pulled into a driveway to turn around, then headed towards the grocery store near Friday Harbor.

Morgan was able to make her way through the store quickly. She was seething, so it was lucky no one tried to talk to her.

What did she expect from him? How could she have been silly enough to be excited about their "date?" Embarrassingly, part of her hoped to see him at the coffee shop. She foolishly bought the story that he liked her and...

Ugh. She was an idiot. One minute he was telling her that he liked her and that he wanted to take her out, and the next minute he was putting the moves on one of their clients! *In public!*

Morgan went to a self check-out so she wouldn't have to make conversation with anyone. Mainly she was angry at herself – Luke was behaving as he always did. But Morgan – she was dumb enough to think that he actually liked her. She didn't think of herself as someone with a big ego, so it took a lot for her to even believe that he'd be interested in her.

Clearly that was a mistake.

She got home and unpacked the groceries, sure that she would have a message from Luke trying to "explain" what he did. She'd already decided that she was going to ignore him and the next time they were together, she'd act like nothing happened. That was the professional thing to do.

After deciding not to open the new ice cream she'd bought, Morgan pulled her phone out of her purse and was hit with a new outrage – he hadn't even *tried* to contact her! So now she couldn't even ignore him!

The nerve!

She told herself that it didn't matter. What was important now was getting back to work – she needed to finish editing some photographs. She made a cup of tea, turned her phone on silent, and got her laptop.

With a bit of music, she was able to focus. But a half-hour into her work, there was a knock at the door. Morgan hopped out of her chair – she was expecting a delivery for a new pair of jeans that she ordered online. That would surely cheer her up.

However, when she opened the door, she found Luke standing there.

"Please – don't shut the door in my face."

Morgan suppressed a smile. She would never shut the door in someone's face, but in this moment, the idea of doing that to him was amusing.

"Hi Luke, how are you?" she said coolly.

"Not good!" he replied. "That woman plotted a meeting so she could attack me!"

Morgan crossed her arms. "Have you spent all this time coming up with that story?"

"No, it's the truth, I swear it. You can ask Marcus. He was there for everything."

Morgan uncrossed her arms. For some reason, that hadn't even crossed her mind as a possibility. And if this woman really *was* harassing Luke, that was pretty terrible. "Well – are you still going to do the video for her?"

"I don't know! I was trying to think what you would do – you know, what the professional thing to do is."

"Well..." Morgan frowned. "I've had people be mean to me and stuff, but no one's ever actually made me feel uncomfortable."

Luke waved a hand. "Oh, I'm not uncomfortable. I don't think that these two should be getting married and she's clearly a sneaky cheater, but I feel like loads of the couples that we meet shouldn't get married."

"Do you want to come in, or just keep standing in the doorway?"

"I would love to come in."

Morgan took a seat on the couch and Luke followed suit.

"So what should I do?"

Morgan shrugged. "I mean – what happened?"

"She sent me an email that said Jackie did her engagement pictures, and she was looking forward to working with me."

"Okay."

"And she said that she looked me up and saw some of the pre-wedding interview videos I'd done, and she'd love to have one made."

"Alright, and then what."

"Well, I invited her to the coffee shop, and I showed her a video – and before this, she was being a bit weird, but I thought she was just a strange person – but when the video was over, she grabbed my hand and said something about what artistic work I did with my strong hands."

Morgan nodded. "Right."

"And that's when you showed up!"

"So I ruined it?"

"No! It's just that – I went to talk to you, and when you left, she was still waiting for me. So I finished the meeting, and she didn't touch me anymore. But she gave me a very creepy vibe and – well I guess she did hug me when she left."

"Sure, and was that when you made plans to take her out on Saturday?"

He frowned. "What? No. Why would I want to see her on Saturday? Or ever again, actually. If you said we should cancel working her wedding, I would be all for it."

Morgan felt the flame of her temper fizzling away. Maybe she'd been a bit harsh. It would be dumb of him to take a client to the coffee shop where he worked and openly hit on her. She just lost her cool when she saw their hands all cozied up...

"I mean, that's up to you." She paused. "I think we'd get a pretty nasty review from her if we canceled so close to her wedding."

"I didn't think of that."

"At the same time, if I were being harassed by the groom, for example, I would like the option to back out of the wedding. So it's really up to you."

Luke sat back and crossed his arms. "I don't so much care about the harassment – I care that *you* know it was harassment."

Morgan got up and walked to the kitchen. Even if Luke was telling the truth, it didn't change the fact of who he was. Did she really expect a peacock to change his feathers?

"Do you want something to drink?" she called out.

"Are you avoiding the question?"

"I'm not, I'm just – I'm thirsty."

"I booked a sunset kayak tour for us on Friday," Luke said, following her into the kitchen. "I really hope that this won't spoil it."

"Sunset kayak tour – how romantic. Do you take all of your dates on sunset tours, or do you generally reserve that for clients?"

"Morgan..."

She turned around to see him standing there, stony faced. He looked genuinely sad; she was a bit surprised. He couldn't possibly be *that* manipulative, could he? As much as she didn't want to be taken for a ride, she also didn't want to hurt his feelings.

"I'm sorry," she said. "I just..."

"You don't trust me."

Morgan felt a blush creeping up her neck and onto her cheeks. "I never said that."

"You don't have to. Listen – let's go kayaking. I'll be a perfect gentleman, and if you have a nice time, I have a really cool place we can go next weekend."

"Oh?" She turned back around to pour herself a glass of iced tea.

"I happen to have an invitation to *the* fundraiser of the year. Hosted by Brock Hunter."

Morgan froze. "You know Brock?"

"Of course, I know everybody."

"What kind of fundraiser? Where is it?"

"It's at his house – well, his mansion really. It's very near Cattle Point, I think you'd like it, the views are spectacular."

Oh, Morgan knew *exactly* where that mansion was. It was a place she was *explicitly* told not to try breaking into again. But if she could walk in, invited? Who knew what she would find – maybe something to finally crack her mom's case.

"That sounds pretty cool," she replied, trying to keep her tone casual.

"Is that a yes?"

Morgan shrugged. "Sure. It's a yes."

Luke clapped his hands together. "I'll text you the details so you can get excited. And so that you can get the right attire – this is a swanky event and we'll have every chance to pretend to be fancy."

"Sure. I'll try not to trash it up."

He frowned. "I didn't mean it like that."

"I know," she said with a laugh. She was kidding. Sort of. Was digging in someones garbage considered trashy? Even if it was for a good cause?

The front door opened and Jade walked in.

"You're home early!" Morgan called out.

"Hey! Yeah – I just had a meeting that I decided to go in for."

Luke popped his head from around the corner. "Hi Jade."

"Oh hi Luke! I'll be right back." Jade disappeared, carrying her work bag into her bedroom.

Luke turned to Morgan. "Do you think that Jade would like to go to the party too?"

A flash of panic ran through Morgan's mind. Jade definitely wouldn't let her go to Brock's house. "No – I don't think so. And...I'd really like it to be just you and me."

"Oh, alright. Well I didn't mean to drop in on you like this – I'll get going. But is it okay if I ask flirty Jillian to communicate with you for all remaining planning?"

"Sure, that seems like a good idea."

"Thank you. I'll see you Friday."

"See you then!"

Morgan saw him out and locked the door. She needed to keep him away from Jade before this party. And she needed to prepare and to get an idea of what she was snooping for. Her mind was so full of ideas that she didn't dwell on Luke hitting on – or being hit on by– that client.

It didn't matter. Luke was right – she didn't trust him. And letting her guard down was a risky move that she wouldn't let happen again.

Chapter 16

The sound of the front door opening carried through the house and Jade stood, listening to hear that Luke left. She didn't want to be an awkward third wheel to Morgan and Luke. Unlike Jade and her never-ending divorce, Morgan didn't have a ton of emotional baggage. There was a real chance that things could work out for them. Jade was happy for them, and wanted to hear how things were going, but she hated having to talk about her own miserable love life.

Morgan asked about the divorce all the time – things like what her lawyer was doing, what the next steps were, how negotiations were going – all of it. Jade knew that Morgan was just being polite; who would want to hear about that awful stuff? She felt ashamed sharing any of it, and the longer it dragged on, the more alone she felt.

As much as Morgan liked to joke about her temper and all of her flaws, they were nothing compared to Jade's failings. She was the first among her siblings to marry, and the first to divorce.

The first failure.

"Hey Jade!" Morgan called out. "I got all of the ingredients we need for dinner."

"Oh great! I'll be out in a second."

Jade turned and looked at herself in the mirror. There were bags under her eyes – she'd had trouble sleeping the previous two nights because she was dreading the meeting with Brandon and their lawyers that evening.

All of the meetings were tense and they never seemed to make much progress. Jade was happy to agree to whatever Brandon wanted, but as soon as she did, he came up with new requests.

She closed her eyes and took a deep breath; there was no need to dump this all onto Morgan – she didn't need to know what an embarrassment Jade's marriage was. After a moment, she opened her eyes, straightened her hair in the mirror, and walked out of her room.

"Thanks for getting all of that stuff, let me know how much I owe you."

Morgan shrugged. "It's on me. Because you will have to do about eighty percent of the cooking."

"Okay," Jade said with a smile. "Deal. Why was Luke here?"

Morgan groaned. "It's a long story. And as usual, I think I've embarrassed myself."

"Why? What happened?"

Morgan rubbed her face with her hands. "After dinner, when he drove me home? He was being really weird. He said that he likes me and that he wanted to take me on a date..."

Jade laughed. "And why is that weird?"

"Because Luke is like – I don't know. I think he does that with all of the girls."

Jade frowned. "He's never said those things to me."

"You know what I mean," Morgan replied. "And I agreed to go on a date with him on Friday, but then I saw him doing something questionable, and I think that it was all a mistake, and mainly, that I'm an idiot."

"You're not an idiot."

"That's very nice of you, but I am. What do *you* think about him?"

"I mean..." Jade paused. What could she possibly say? What if she gave Morgan bad advice and sentenced her to a never ending horrible divorce too? "I don't think that I can be the authority on men. I have a poor track record and shouldn't be trusted."

"Oh come on," said Morgan, wrapping Jade in a hug. "That was just one guy. Just *one* mistake!"

Jade felt her cheeks reddening. "It was a big enough mistake. So I dunno – obviously you don't know Luke well, but he was nice at dinner. And you guys were being all – cute together."

"What do you mean *cute*?"

"I mean, you know – you were teasing each other, and being funny, and it just seemed like you really jived. Plus he's handsome, and *that accent...*"

Morgan shut her eyes. "I *know*, the accent is ridiculous. I hate to admit it, but I see what other girls see in him."

"What a shining endorsement."

"Well – whatever." Morgan busied herself with putting away some clean dishes. "I guess we'll see. What time do you want to have dinner tonight?"

"I have to meet with Brandon at six..."

Morgan's smile faded. "Oh, right. That stinks. Do you want me to come with you?"

"No, but thanks," Jade said, shaking her head. "I'm just going to get the marinade going for the chicken before I go. And when I get back we can finish up?"

"Sure, that works for me."

Jade welcomed the chance to do something to take her mind off of the sick feeling in the pit of her stomach. The recipe was uncomplicated – she'd found it online – but she wasn't completely comfortable with grilling, so that would be a new experience.

She mixed the ingredients, cut up the chicken, and set it in the fridge. Morgan was already back in her room, working on editing pictures from her last wedding. Jade was impressed with Morgan for building a new life for herself. It made her feel a certain way – she paused to try to pin the feeling down.

It wasn't jealousy – not in a malicious sense. But Jade felt so broken and lost...sometimes she felt like she was so low that she could only look up and admire all that Morgan was doing, and that she'd never be there herself. The longer that the divorce went on, the more certain she felt that she'd never be happy again. Who would want to date a late twenties divorcée? How would she even explain that?

Jade quickly changed her outfit before getting in the car to drive to her lawyer's office. For once, Brandon agreed to come to San Juan Island to meet – normally, Jade had to meet him in Anacortes. She made the trip without music, trying to steady her nerves.

Brandon never looked uncomfortable during these meetings, yet no matter how much Jade tried to psych herself up to look poised and confident, it never worked. Her insides squirmed, her body felt unusually cold, and she generally felt like the helpless prey of a large animal.

She got to her lawyer's office and was shown to the conference room. Normally she declined their offer for something to drink, but today she decided to take some tea to warm up her hands. Her lawyer Corey came in with the tea after a few minutes.

"So I think I may have figured out why Brandon has been expanding on his demands."

Jade accepted the mug, wrapping both of her hands around it. "Oh?"

"It's not great news...apparently, he got elective shoulder surgery last week."

"Ah. I know that his shoulder has always bothered him."

Corey nodded. "And with the way the divorce is currently set, he's still on your insurance."

Jade nodded. "Right."

"And..." Corey let out a sigh. "You'll be responsible for paying the deductible and coinsurance for the surgery."

"Oh." Jade sat for a moment to absorb this information. "I have to say, I didn't see this coming. Do you know how much it'll be?"

Corey shook his head. "It depends on your insurance and what the deductible is, what your copay is, all of that stuff."

Jade frowned. She was pretty sure that her deductible for the two of them was something like $5,000 every year. "Wow. That is really bad news..."

"But I think now we can really push for the end of all of this."

Jade nodded and tried to take a sip of her tea; she felt overpowered with nausea.

The conference room door opened and Brandon walked in with his lawyer Carla.

Corey stood up to shake their hands. "Evening, nice to see you."

"Take it easy," said Brandon. "I'm still recovering."

Oh dear, he was *not* in a good mood. Jade nodded a hello, which he didn't see. Or maybe he ignored it.

Corey cleared his throat. "Things are coming along well, I think to get started –"

Brandon interrupted. "I really don't appreciate that you made me come all the way out here when I'm still injured."

"Thanks again for making the trip," Corey said with a smile. "We appreciate it. I was made aware that –"

"I'm serious, I'm not coming out here again," Brandon reiterated.

"Let's just let him say what he needs to say," Jade said in a small voice.

Brandon narrowed his eyes. "Oh I'm sorry, I thought this was between you and me?"

"Please don't raise your voice," said Jade. "We won't make you come out here again."

"And," added Corey, "if we can get things moving, maybe we won't even *have* to meet again."

"I think we'd be happy to work towards that," replied Carla, a broad smile on her face.

Brandon scoffed. "You don't even care that I'm injured and can't work. You just want to cut me off."

Injured? Was this his next ploy? That he was unable to work and that she needed to support him indefinitely? The only reason Brandon didn't work was because he didn't *want* to work.

Jade felt herself growing annoyed. She would have to clear out most of her savings to pay for his surgery; how was he okay with that? Didn't he realize that she had a life, too? And that she was more than just a paycheck?

She reminded herself to stay calm, but she couldn't sit there silently and let him flaunt this attitude.

"Eventually you'll need to find a way to support yourself, Brandon. I know it'll be hard, but it'll be good for you."

Brandon stood up. "Are you *kidding* me? Good for me?"

A chill went down her back. Maybe she shouldn't have said that. Brandon couldn't handle criticism, and he definitely didn't like being told what was good for him.

Why did she say that?

"You make a *ton* of money!" Brandon's voice boomed. "I've been your moral support all of these years. And now you want to abandon me? You ungrateful –"

"Brandon, let's sit down," Carla said. "I know you're uncomfortable and this is hard on you."

He nodded towards her. "I *am* uncomfortable, you're right, I shouldn't have to deal with this."

Jade shot a worried glance at Corey. Her back hurt from leaning so hard into her chair. "I don't have tons of money, Brandon. You know that, and we can't go on like this forever."

"This is ridiculous! And you're right, we're getting nowhere. I can't believe you expect me to work like this."

A drop of spit flew from his mouth and landed on the table in front of her. She decided to keep her eyes focused on it instead of him.

He crossed his arms and shook his head. "You *know* that I've been trying to make it as a DJ, and now that I'm at a really crucial time in my career, you're going to just pull the rug out from under me?"

"Brandon," Jade said, trying to soften her voice. "I don't want to do that, but it's been a year and I think we should –"

"Seriously Jade, how could you?" He stood up again, his voice roaring across the room. "Don't you know that this is how people get desperate? If you just toss me out like this, with nothing, who knows what I could do? I can't be held responsible if something bad happens."

"Brandon, let's have a seat and talk this out," Carla sputtered.

Brandon ignored her, leaning forward until he was only a few inches from Jade's face. "Like I could *literally* starve to death, and you don't even care! If you take everything away from me, I don't know what I'll do."

Jade stared at him, unable to move. What was that supposed to mean?

Carla reached to grab Brandon's arm, but he yanked it away.

"No, I'm serious!" he said, voice cracking. "If you do this, I don't even know what to say. I mean, I've been really good about everything. Even when you decided to leave me, totally out of the blue. And now, if you dump me like a piece of trash – I don't know! You're forcing me into desperation. And I don't *want* to do this, but it's not like I don't know where you live, and I'm going to end up hurting you, Jade. I don't *want* to do that, but that's what's going to happen."

"One moment," Corey said, "did you say you're going to hurt Jade?"

Carla didn't have a chance to stop him – Brandon responded instantly. "I have no other choice! This is what she's forcing me to do! She is *forcing* me into a corner, and it's like – well, I'm like a cornered lion. I'll attack, I *will* attack."

"Alright, we cannot have your client threatening to harm my client," said Corey, clasping his hands together.

"Oh, okay, so now you're going to hide behind your expensive lawyer? Don't you think he's a little old to be your boyfriend?"

Jade placed a hand over her eyes. "Brandon, you just need to –"

"You don't tell me what I *need* to do!"

Every muscle in Jade's body was taut. She stared at him, afraid to say anything. She'd never known him to be like this – so aggressive. He could be rude or whiny, and sure, sometimes when he was frustrated he'd throw things. But nothing like this, and never directed at her.

Jade listened to her heart pounding in her chest; it made her breathing feel unnatural. She would give him whatever he wanted if he'd just leave her alone.

There was a murmur outside of the door and Jade heard the sound of a muted voice over a walkie-talkie. A moment later, Matthew walked into the conference room.

Jade gaped at him, mouth slightly open. Was she hallucinating?

"I got a call about a disturbance," said Matthew.

Jade wished that she could melt into a puddle and hide under the table. Matthew moved quickly, right toward Brandon. She prayed that he wouldn't see her, but at that exact moment, their eyes met.

She looked away. It was bad enough that the lawyers were here to witness this – why did Matthew have to be here too?

"Thanks for coming officer," Corey stood. "We've been going through some divorce disagreements, and this man threatened to hurt my client if he didn't get what he wanted."

"Give me a break," Brandon spat out. "This is ridiculous, I clearly can't hurt anyone. My arm is in a sling. I'm just saying if I have no other choice, then that's what *will* happen. They're being overly sensitive. You're dismissed officer."

Matthew raised an eyebrow. "What was the nature of this threat?"

Jade took in a breath to say something, but Brandon shot her a glare. She sunk down into her chair.

"This is all a misunderstanding, things get heated sometimes," explained Carla.

Corey nodded. "Yes, they do. Which is why we have a button under the desk to call the police if things get *too* heated. I'm willing to give a statement."

"Oh come on!" Brandon protested, throwing his good arm in the air.

"Thank you very much," said Matthew, and in one quick motion, he grabbed Brandon's good arm, spun him around and started walking him out.

Brandon yelped. "This is police brutality! I'm an injured man!"

"Well injured man, let me remind you that you have the right to remain silent."

Brandon whimpered. "Ow! Stop it! Please, let me go, my wife is a –"

"*Silent*," Matthew reiterated as he pushed Brandon out of the room.

Carla let out a sigh and rubbed her forehead. "Oh boy. I'll be talking to you later."

"Good luck with that one." Corey said with a laugh. "I have a feeling that our frequent meetings are about to come to an end."

"What do you mean?" asked Jade.

"Well, it looks like you'll have the chance to press charges against him. And I think having that hanging over his head will force him to be a lot more cooperative."

"Oh." Jade stood up, feeling a bit dizzy from all that just happened. She put a hand on the table to support herself.

"I'll be in contact later this week, okay?" said Corey. "Don't worry. Why don't you head home and get some rest?"

Jade nodded. She didn't want to go outside and run into Matthew, so instead she excused herself to the restroom and wasted ten minutes before slipping into the parking lot.

Unfortunately, Matthew was still there, taking a statement from Corey. When he spotted her, he walked over immediately.

"Are you okay?" he asked.

Jade nodded. "Yeah, of course. I appreciate that you got here so quickly."

Matthew nodded. "It was no problem. I was just up the street actually. I think the front end staff called when the button was pressed."

"That's good. It was very nice of you to come and – I'm so sorry, I have to go."

Jade rushed to her car, hot tears about to spill down her cheeks. She was able to get to her car before anything escaped, and she pulled away without looking back.

Chapter 17

That night, Morgan didn't hear when Jade returned home; she was too focused on the pictures that she was editing, and her music was a bit loud. It wasn't until she heard the shower turn on that she realized Jade was back.

She checked her phone and saw that Jade sent a text asking to push grilling back until tomorrow. That seemed odd, but she responded that she was okay with that plan.

After her shower, Jade didn't stop in to say hello or anything, so before getting ready for bed, Morgan decided to check on her. She crept up to her bedroom door and softly knocked.

"Are you okay in there?" Morgan asked.

"Oh yeah – I'm fine. I'm just going to turn in early tonight."

Hm. Jade's voice sounded...off.

"Did everything go okay with the lawyers?"

Silence.

After a moment, Jade responded. "It wasn't great."

"Do you want to talk about it?"

"No, not right now. But thank you."

"Okay. Well...have a good night."

"You too."

Morgan had to resist the urge to barge into Jade's room; clearly Jade wanted some alone time. Morgan knew that she'd be able to get the story out of her eventually. It might take a month, but it would happen. That was usually how long Jade took to share how she was feeling – if not longer.

Morgan let out a sigh. She had all the time in the world to wait. She went to the kitchen, refilled her glass of water, and got ready for bed.

The rest of the week went by quickly; she finished editing all of the pictures that she had in her work queue and met with several potential clients. She also had the pleasure of corresponding with Jillian several times. That woman was *pushy*, insisting that she needed to talk to Luke directly to "flesh out" her "ideal vision."

It appeared more and more likely that Luke was telling the truth. After Jillian's third email about the "importance of lens range and mood," Morgan considered telling her that their professional relationship wasn't going to work out. Yet her dread of a bad review from an enraged Jillian prevented her from fully canceling the blessed event.

For the entire week, Morgan tried to think of excuses to get out of her date with Luke, but she couldn't come up with anything. Eventually she resigned herself to going on the date for the sake of keeping her invite to Brock's party.

By Friday afternoon, Morgan was scrambling to pull together the gear she needed for kayaking. Jade generously offered to loan her a rain jacket.

"Oh," Jade said as she handed it over, "is this for your date with Luke?"

"It is." Morgan debated complaining about the date, but decided against it. Jade still seemed pretty down, and it wasn't appropriate to whine about having to go on a date when Jade had so much more going on.

"Well that should be fun. And I think this jacket is mostly waterproof," Jade said. "And sorry about the color – I got it on sale."

Morgan pulled on the mustard yellow jacket and studied herself in the mirror. "Thank you! It's perfect."

Morgan made sure to get into town early; she wanted to scope out this kayak place and decide if they were in good hands. She was surprised to find that Luke was already there. He waved at her as soon as she walked in.

"Hey! You made it."

Morgan smiled – was he surprised that she showed up?

"I did."

"Do you have everything that you need? Water shoes, rain jacket, life jacket?"

Morgan paused. "Uh – I was supposed to bring my own life jacket?"

He laughed. "No – I'm just joking about that. But we can find one that fits you – just here in this other room."

Morgan nodded. "Alright."

"Also," he said as he led her to the back of the store. "I took the liberty of packing us some snacks, so I hope you're hungry. And that you like fancy cheese."

"Oh – thanks. That sounds nice."

Morgan pretended like she was focusing on the life jackets, but really her head was spinning. What had gotten into him? Why was he acting like this? He was being nice...*overly* nice. Was it possible that he knew about Brock's connection to her mother? Did Brock put him up to this? Was she walking into some sort of trap? How did he even know Brock?

"Okay everyone," said the young guy at the front of the shop. "My name is Reg and I'll be your tour guide today. If you could please gather around and I'll go over some of the basics."

Morgan studied him; he couldn't have been much older than she was, and naturally, this worried her. How could he possibly know what he was doing? Did he know how to navigate the ocean? Like *really* navigate, or would he lead them crashing into some rocks and they would be lost forever?

Actually...maybe that was how people felt when they met her, too, and she promised to take beautiful pictures of their weddings. They probably thought she had no idea what she was doing. And they were kind of right.

She scoffed and Luke shot her a look.

Whoops. Morgan made a mental note to try to make herself look older. Then she took a deep breath to snap out of her wandering mind and force herself to listen to Reg's instructions.

She was able to listen for about thirty seconds before her eyes drifted onto the other people on the tour – it seemed they'd be spending the evening with two couples. One couple was older, probably in their fifties. They both stood straight, listening intently. The other couple was younger and Morgan pegged them as newlyweds.

"Alright, so if you'd all like to come over to the van, we'll drive over to the launch point."

Uh oh – Morgan completely missed *all* of the instructions. Hopefully Luke was paying attention. She turned to him and offered a brief smile and he smiled back.

"Well this is going to be quite an adventure, don't you think?"

"Yeah, definitely. Let me know how much I owe you for this so I can pay you back."

"My invitation, my treat," he said, holding the door open for her.

"No – really I just –"

"After you Miss Allen."

She smiled at him before walking through the door. Something was definitely up with him. Maybe this *was* all a ploy...

The launch point for the kayaks was a short drive away, and everyone in the van chatted pleasantly. Morgan didn't say much, but she listened. She was right about the young couple – they'd just gotten married the month prior, and she knew this because Carmen, the bride, insisted on showing everyone her wedding pictures.

"Oh, look at that lighting!" Luke gushed, pausing on a particularly dark picture.

"I know," Carmen cooed. "My photographer told me that she didn't even need a flash for some of the dark pictures. They look amazing!"

"Remarkable," Luke said, not breaking eye contact with Morgan.

Morgan had to turn toward the window so she wouldn't crack up. She felt bad that Luke was making fun of the girl, but at the same time, she *was* forcing a van full of strangers to look at her wedding pictures. And she didn't seem to notice that Luke was making fun of her, which was sort of a blessing.

Carmen wasn't able to get through all of the pictures before Reg stopped the van and opened the side door.

"Okay, so what I'll have you do is each take one end of your kayak and walk it just down there to the shore."

The older couple went first, then Morgan and Luke.

Carmen stood, arms crossed. "Can't someone else carry this? I didn't pay for *this* kind of a tour."

Luke, dutifully carrying the front end of their kayak, turned around to make a face. "I can't believe she didn't book us for her wedding. She seems like a delight and we wouldn't have needed to bring any lights or anything!"

"I know, it would've been a breeze!"

They set their kayak down on the rocky beach, and after a few minutes, Reg carried the last kayak down with the sheepish-faced groom.

"Okay," said Reg, clapping his hands together. "I'm going to help each of you launch your kayaks. Now remember, these are sea kayaks, so it's difficult to tip them over. But I have had one instance where some very persistent kids were able to tip their kayak. Don't be like those kids."

Everyone laughed.

"The person in the front will walk into the water first – have your partner hold the back as you hop in. Remember, whoever is in the back is in charge of steering, so choose wisely."

Morgan and Luke turned to each other; Luke spoke first. "I'm happy to take on the steering responsibility, but I am afraid I might be too big for this kayak in either spot."

Morgan laughed. "I guess we'll find out."

Everyone except the newlyweds carried their kayaks in the water. Morgan could hear the young man pleading with his bride. "You just have to get a *little* bit wet, it won't be that bad!"

"But it's freezing! And my feet will be wet the whole time!"

"She's not wrong," Morgan said under her breath. "But she *is* annoying."

"Exactly," said Luke, holding the kayak steady.

The water was cold, but Morgan found it refreshing. She sloshed through, careful not to slip. It always seemed tempting to go for a swim when she was on one of her hikes, but a single touch of the water quickly changed her mind. The water was just about 50°F – warm enough for the orcas, but not warm enough for her.

Morgan got into her seat and settled in, and Luke followed soon after. They wobbled left and right, but there seemed to be little danger of tipping. It took Luke a few minutes to adjust so he could reach the pedals comfortably, but he was confident he could get the hang of it.

Morgan handed him a paddle and they carefully practiced navigating in the still waters. It took another ten minutes of squealing and whining to get the newlyweds into their kayak.

"And all this time I thought the other couple was going to slow us down," said Luke.

Morgan shook her head. "Apparently they're avid river kayakers. So we'll have to be careful that they don't leave *us* behind."

"How do you know that?"

"They were talking about it in the van."

"Ah," said Luke. "I was very occupied at that time."

Morgan laughed and turned back around to face the front of the kayak. "You were."

Once everyone was finally in the water, Reg swiftly cut ahead of them and led them on a tour down the west coast of the island. Despite zero kayaking experience between the two of them, Luke and Morgan managed to get far enough away from the newlyweds to enjoy the peace of the sea. They glided along the water's glassy surface, and though Morgan knew that her shoulders would be stiff the next day, she didn't mind.

Reg told them that his goal was to get them close to Lime Kiln Park so that they might catch a glimpse of the resident orcas who'd been hunting up and down the coast all day. Morgan wasn't quite sure where they'd launched from, but it seemed quite far from Lime Kiln.

She told herself to enjoy the ride, even though she rather anxiously hoped to see the orcas. Along the way, they spotted harbor seals lounging on rocks, bald eagles circling above and even a porpoise in the distance.

Miraculously, they made it to the Lime Kiln Lighthouse, and Reg encouraged them to take a break and relax.

"Finally!" Luke said. "I get to impress you with my water picnic."

"I can't wait to see what this is."

Luke carefully opened a waterproof bag and handed Morgan a small can of red wine. "Now I also have a chardonnay if you'd prefer, but from what I remember, you seem to like the reds."

"Impressive," said Morgan. "You are right. Thank you."

He reached back into the bag and pulled out a plastic wrapped paper plate with sliced meats and cheeses. "Oh darn – this was laid out so much nicer before, but it got a bit jostled in the bag."

Morgan laughed. "It still looks great."

"But wait! There's more!" Luke reached into the bag and pulled out two separately wrapped small baguettes and a handful of chocolates.

"For dessert," he said.

"This is really way too nice Luke. Thank you."

If he was trying to trick her in some way, he was really going over the top. She tried to push it out of her mind and instead enjoy this small picnic, chatting with the other couples as their kayaks gently rocked on the water. After about half an hour, Reg said that they needed to head back before the sunset so they wouldn't end up kayaking in the dark.

Morgan was disappointed that they hadn't seen any orcas, but she kept that to herself. Carmen was not of the same mindset.

"I thought we were guaranteed to see killer whales," she called out.

"Unfortunately, there are no guarantees in nature," replied Reg. "I'd heard over the radio that the orcas were swimming up and down the coast all day, so I guess we just missed them."

"So I got into this deathtrap and had wet shoes for the last two hours for *nothing*?"

Morgan giggled. Carmen was both annoying and unintentionally funny. Her constant complaints kept Morgan from falling too deep into her own mind. The ocean made her feel small and incomplete for some reason, and she'd rather ignore that feeling at the moment.

"Shall we pick up the pace a bit?" Luke asked.

"Yes, let's. My shoulders are pretty sore, but I'll see what I can do."

"Don't worry. I'm very strong, you know."

Morgan laughed. "Right."

They were able to put some distance between themselves and the other people in the group, but Morgan wanted to make sure that they were still in sight of Reg. The water was calm, but she had no bravado about the ocean and didn't want to tempt fate.

They were almost out of earshot when they first heard something.

"Was that what I think it was?" asked Morgan.

"I'm not sure. It seemed so quiet – could it have been a seal? Or a porpoise?"

Morgan frowned, and squinted across the water. "No! Look there!"

Luke followed her finger to see where she was pointing. "I don't see anything."

"I think they're underwater now – but I'm pretty sure that I just saw the whales."

They sat and frantically scanned the water for another fin. The orcas didn't make them wait long – after just a few moments, they resurfaced and the mist of their breath was unmistakable.

"Oh my gosh!" Morgan almost dropped her paddle as her hands darted to her mouth. "There they are!"

By this point, the older couple caught up to them, but the newlyweds were still quite far behind. They sat together in silence and awe, watching the orcas swim by. They were still quite far off – Morgan guessed that they were at least a hundred feet away – but they could still make them out clearly against the quickly turning sky. After what seemed like no time at all, the orcas were gone, disappearing into the distance.

Morgan squinted into the darkness for a moment before giving up. She had no words, and not even Carmen's high pitched voice could distract her from her thoughts.

All she could think about was whether her mother got a chance to see the killer whales the last time she was on the island. Would there even have been orcas in the month that she visited? How unfair if she'd come all that way and not gotten to see their beauty one last time...

Morgan felt it coming on but couldn't stop it – tears welled in her eyes and her throat grew tight. She put a hand up to her mouth to quiet any sobs that escaped, but one whimper still made it out. She shut her eyes, telling herself to stop this nonsense, but it didn't help.

The older couple, talking animatedly, was already moving on. Morgan fumbled with her oar, but her vision was blurred.

No, no one could see her like this. Acting like a loony. Especially not the guy in the back of the kayak.

Slowly, the kayak turned north. Luke quietly, and seemingly effortlessly, moved them back to rejoin the group.

Chapter 18

Although Matthew tried his best to be on time for his second Sunday dinner at Margie's, a broken down car ruined his plans. It wasn't his – it belonged to a woman who he spotted on the side of the road. He was actually going to get to Margie's ten minutes early before he pulled over to see what was going on.

It ended up being a more heroic reason for being late than the last time – the woman's car had a flat tire, and Matthew helped her change it. It wasn't quite as goofy as the image of him chasing geese around. Jade hadn't said anything about the geese, of course, but Morgan teased him a bit. He didn't mind the teasing, but he really wanted to know what Jade was thinking.

He also wanted to see how Jade was doing after that bizarre encounter with her ex-husband. Or rather, soon to be ex-husband. Matthew took pleasure in booking that jerk and carefully documenting each and every threat that he made against Jade.

How Jade managed to remain stoic around him, Matthew had no idea. But he found himself thinking about her more and more – what other secrets did she hold behind those beautiful eyes?

As soon as he finished changing the tire, he was on his way to find out. He got to Margie's about twenty minutes late; Morgan opened the door to greet him.

"Oh! Hey Matthew, I didn't know you were coming tonight."

"Hey, I'm so sorry, I was actually going to be on time today, but I had to help a lady change a flat tire."

Morgan motioned for him to come in and closed the door behind him. "Likely story Matthew. Saving geese, chasing women."

"That's incorrect – it was chasing geese and saving women."

Morgan laughed and led him into the dining room. "Hey, look who showed up!"

"I am *so* sorry that I'm late, but I brought dessert!"

Margie stood up to give him a hug and accepted his store-bought brownies. "That's very nice of you."

Matthew frowned, looking at the table. There didn't seem to be a place for him; the only places were for Jade, Morgan, and Margie. "I'm so sorry – did Chief not tell you that I'd be coming today?"

"Oh, I guess he didn't mention it, but it's no trouble and you're more than welcome," said Margie as she disappeared into the kitchen.

Oh boy. Now he'd really done it – not only did he invite himself over for dinner, he then showed up late and spoiled everyone's evening.

He took a step back. "You know what, I'm so sorry, I should probably go."

Jade's eyes darted up to him. "No – you should stay. Really."

He hesitated for a moment and Morgan grabbed him by the wrist. "Come on, don't be shy, have a seat."

Morgan led him to a chair – she was surprisingly strong for so small a person – and he took a seat across from Jade.

"It's nice to see you again," he said.

Jade flashed a smile. "Yes, it's nice to see you too."

Morgan cleared her throat and announced that she was going into the kitchen to help Margie.

"Thank you for your help the other day," said Jade, voice hushed. "I haven't told my mom about all of the commotion yet. I just...haven't found the right words."

Matthew nodded. "Your secret is safe with me. But I want you to know – I took very careful notes of everything he said. And I'm more than happy to testify or make a statement on your behalf. Anything you need."

"Thank you." Jade stared at him for a moment before looking away.

Matthew smiled back; he was happy to have the excuse to be able to look at her. He was transfixed – her long hair, her delicate hands. Those beautiful green eyes...

Morgan and Margie reentered the room carrying a large casserole dish.

"This is my *very* special baked ziti," Margie said.

Morgan clapped her hands together. "Oh my gosh, this is one of my favorites. Where's Chief? He's going to be really mad that he missed out on this."

"Oh, I don't know..." Margie said airily as she removed her apron.

Jade cocked her head slightly to the side. "Is he sick or something?"

Margie sighed. "Well – I didn't know how to tell you this, girls. And Matthew – I guess you should hear, too."

His stomach dropped – he had no idea what was going on, but he knew it wasn't good.

Margie continued. "Hank and I are taking a little...break."

Morgan gasped. "What? Why?"

"We both decided that it was the best decision for everyone, and –"

"You mean the best decision for Amanda," Jade said softly, setting down her napkin.

"Honey, please don't be angry with her. She's just a young woman struggling with the loss of her mother, and I don't want to –"

"I don't care *what* she's struggling with if she ruins *my* mom's happiness."

Matthew felt like an animal trapped in a cage. His eyes darted between Jade, Morgan and Margie. Should he say something? Should he silently get up and leave? No – that wouldn't work.

Margie scooped a large spoonful of ziti onto Jade's plate. "You'll understand one day."

"I don't think I will," Jade said.

Even though she wasn't yelling or even raising her voice, Matthew felt the heavy weight behind her words.

Morgan threw her hands in the air "This is ridiculous. What's Amanda's number? I need to talk to her."

Margie covered her eyes with her hand. "Morgan – I know that you want to help, but please just sit down and eat."

Morgan sat down without another word. For a few moments, the only sounds were forks and knives scraping against plates.

Matthew had to lighten the mood. "Yesterday I got a call about a guy running around in his underwear."

"Oh?" said Margie.

"Yes, I got a distressed call because a lady thought he was some sort of a maniac. I found him pretty fast – he was right up by Fourth of July beach. Apparently he thought it would be a good idea to go for a swim, so he took all his clothes off, got one foot in the water, and then changed his mind. But his friends had already made off with his clothes and drove away, so he was stuck running around in his – you know, underwear."

"You've got some really strange stories Matthew," Morgan said flatly. "Do you ever do any regular police stuff?"

Matthew laughed. He didn't mind being the butt of the joke if it would change the tone of the conversation. He shot a look at Jade and saw that she had a smile on her lips. "Sure, lots of it is boring. Or dealing with your run-of-the-mill jerks."

Morgan nodded, taking a sip of water. "Right. But you didn't get into it for that. You got into it for the wild goose chases."

"Domesticated goose chases, but yes."

The rest of dinner carried on about the same, with Matthew trying to tell funny stories, and everyone else somewhat participating. At the end, Margie and Jade cleared the table and Morgan pulled him aside.

"I need to ask two favors of you."

He raised his eyebrows. "Why do I feel this is going to get me in trouble?"

"Ignore that feeling. Listen – I need you to distract Margie for like two minutes so that I can get Amanda's number from her phone."

"Oh – I don't know if –"

"Just say yes. Say it. Tell me you'll help. Say yes."

"Okay, I guess," Matthew said, trying not to laugh. "But this never gets back to Chief."

Morgan waved a hand. "Let me handle him."

"And what's the second favor?"

"Well," Morgan leaned in and lowered her voice. "Even though I like to joke around, I really am interested in the work that you do."

"Okay?"

"And there's actually a case that I wish I could help with. I did a ride along with Chief one time, you know. And there was a woman involved in a hit-and-run, and I've become somewhat of a car expert, and I think that –"

"Morgan, I'm not going to show you any of the evidence from my cases. And especially not *that* case."

She stared at him for a beat before apparently giving up. "Fine. But you'll help me with Margie?"

"I'll help you with Margie."

They went into the kitchen and Matthew managed to ask Margie enough questions about the view out of the kitchen window for Morgan to sneak around behind them and get the number she wanted.

After that, he decided he'd trespassed on their hospitality long enough and it was time for him to get going. He thanked them for the nice evening and saw himself out.

When he got back to his car, he sat and absorbed the silence for a moment. That was the last time he was showing up *anywhere* unannounced.

Chapter 19

The week after their kayaking date, all Luke could think about was Morgan. Unfortunately, they didn't have any jobs to do together for a while. That Sunday, Luke left for a two day shoot on the mainland for a car dealership, and when he got back, Morgan was busy editing photographs and doing family photo shoots. Luke thought about showing up and volunteering to help, but he didn't want to be weird.

Perhaps it was best to put some distance between them – people always said that absence made the heart grow fonder, right? It was definitely working on his heart; the effect on Morgan's heart remained to be seen.

She got emotional at the end of the kayak trip, seemingly out of nowhere. Luke had no idea what that was about – he wanted to offer some comfort, but he didn't know what to say, and he also didn't want to make her talk in front of those idiot newlyweds. Then, as soon as he got them back to shore, she was back to normal again.

Were they tears of joy? That seemed rather...wholesome. And sweet. Not that Morgan *wasn't* sweet, but that was such an innocent thing to do. No – she wasn't the kind of person to cry tears of joy.

No matter! He would find some way to bring it up to her, maybe at Uncle Brock's party. After some time passed, he might even be able to joke with her about it and get to the truth.

He could almost envision it; Morgan could be incredibly serious but a moment later, she'd turn it on him with sarcasm. She was different than anyone he'd met before – oddest of all, she looked at *him* differently, and therefore didn't see what everyone else thought they saw.

He found himself daydreaming about seeing her again; he'd been texting her all week, just to make sure she didn't have time to back out of her agreement to be his date to the party.

Friday evening, Luke went to the pub with his roommates for trivia night. Matthew asked if he could join, which was perfect, because Steve was out of town and they needed at least four for a team.

"So Luke," Brad said as he leaned his elbows onto the table. "Is this mysterious Morgan coming tonight too?"

"Not that I know of. Why?"

Larry laughed. "Because Brad is still mad that you stole Macy and he wants to steal this girl you've been talking about nonstop as payback."

"Listen Bradley," Luke said, unable to contain his smirk. "I declined Macy's invitation and sent her your way. Surely you don't expect me to ask her out for you as well."

"It's not that easy!" Brad shot him an annoyed look. "I can't just walk up to her and say 'Hey you want to go for a bike ride?' It doesn't work like that!"

Luke shrugged. "What if I promised you that it did?"

"And what if she said no?"

"Well – then you move on."

Brad shook his head. "Nah – she's the one for me. I can feel it. It's a matter of time. I think she'll come to me."

"Alright then."

Luke smiled to himself. Brad was the quintessential single guy. He was quite desperately looking for love – always looking, but never acting. No matter how much they encouraged him, or tried to help him, or talk to girls with him, Brad was frozen with fear. It seemed odd to Luke – Brad just needed to take a chance.

"So Matthew," Larry said, "Have you met this mysterious Morgan?"

Matthew smiled. "I have."

"Really? I thought Luke made her up because none of us have ever seen her before."

Luke couldn't stop himself. "That's because she has a business to run."

Matthew laughed. "You actually kind of sounded like her there."

Larry stood up and pointed at them both. "I'm going to get a drink, do you guys want anything?"

"I'll go with you," said Brad. "We can walk around the bar and see who's here."

Larry shot Luke a pleading look, but consigned himself to going on this "mission" with Brad. Luke watched as they slowly took the long way around, Brad's scowl likely scaring away anyone who might want to talk to them.

"So," Matthew leaned forward. "I missed you at Sunday dinner this week."

"Oh, you went to Margie's? I'm sorry I missed it, I had to shoot a video of one of those long-armed mascots at a car dealership. A tube man, I think they call it? It was extremely windy and it kept being blown out of my shot. Have you ever seen one of those things? They're atrocious."

Matthew nodded. "Yeah, those are pretty common in the states. And that sounds rough. Maybe not as rough as the dinner, though."

"Why? What happened?"

Oh no. Had Luke made Morgan cry for some reason, and she was complaining about him at dinner? What an idiot he'd been. Why hadn't he asked her what was wrong sooner? She didn't hint that anything was wrong between them. And Morgan wasn't one to be subtle.

"Apparently Margie and Chief Hank are taking a break."

"Oh." Well that wasn't so bad! But it might explain why Morgan was crying.

"And Margie waited to drop *that* bomb until Jade and Morgan kept asking where he was. Oh – and because he wasn't there, he didn't tell Margie that I was coming."

Ah, so Morgan didn't know about that yet. Not the cause of her crying. "Wow. You win. That sounds much more difficult to handle than a single tube man."

"I wouldn't call it a disaster," Matthew replied, shaking his head. "But it was touch and go there for a bit. And then Morgan tried to trick me into showing her a bunch of evidence from her mom's case."

"You have a case open against her mother?"

Morgan's mom was a *criminal*? Actually...that kind of made sense.

Matthew shook his head. "Not against her – about her death."

"Wait, hold on. I knew that her mom passed away, but –"

"She didn't tell you?" Matthew sat back in his chair. "Her mom was killed by a hit-and-run driver last year."

"You're joking! Here on the island?"

"Yeah, and they thought they had a good lead at first, but it went cold. And Chief Hank gave me the case to see if I could help figure it out."

"And did you?"

"Not yet. We've got a lot of circumstantial evidence, but nothing solid. Nothing we can really go on. A bumper was left behind at the scene to a car we know belonged to a collector on the island. But we can't prove that it was him, and he's lawyered up."

Luke felt a chill run down his neck. "Oh? My uncle is part of that car scene. Perhaps I know the guy?"

"You might, I hear he's a jerk though. His name is Brock – Brock Hunter."

Luke felt his jaw tighten. "I do know him. And yes, he's a jerk."

Matthew sighed. "And there's a lot that happened – the car disappeared and Brock was caught driving drunk, but we couldn't get him for that. And then Morgan went around harassing people and trying to get video footage of the night that her mom was hit. And unbelievably, someone came forward with a video."

"And that didn't give you enough evidence?"

"Nope. It just made things more complicated, because it wasn't Brock driving the car. But I really shouldn't be talking about this – I don't want you to run and tell Morgan everything." Matthew looked over his shoulder and leaned forward. "When she found out about the car, she showed up on the island and tried to break into Brock's garage."

Luke buried his face in his hands. "Stop. You have to stop. Matthew – I know Brock *really* well."

Matthew frowned. "Oh – I'm sorry. Is he a friend of yours?"

"Not exactly. I just – I can't wrap my head around what you're telling me."

"Listen, I shouldn't have said any of that. Please don't tell Morgan – or Brock. Like I said, we don't have anything."

"Don't worry, your secret is safe with me."

Matthew nodded. "I'm going to get another beer, do you want anything?"

"No thanks, I'm fine."

Luke forced himself to smile to ease Matthew's worries, but he was *far* from fine. He needed to find a way to back out of taking Morgan to that party, and he needed to find it *now*.

Chapter 20

"What do you think of this one?" Morgan popped out of her bedroom to show Jade the new red dress she'd ordered online.

"Whoa, I like this one! It really makes you stand out!"

Hm. Standing out wasn't exactly what Morgan was going for. "I'm going to text Luke and make sure that I have the right dress code."

Morgan went back into her bedroom and snapped a picture of herself in the mirror. She sent it along to Amanda along with a text that read, "I'm getting ready to go to a party tomorrow. There are times when I miss my mom so much that I don't think that I can function or that anything will be fun ever again. But sometimes I still feel happy, so I let it happen. Is there anything you like to do for fun?"

She read the text back to herself; maybe she was being too forward? Amanda was practically a stranger. But if Chief and Margie *did* get married, she'd be Jade's step-sister, and her... step-step sister? Was that text too much for a step-step sister?

Nah!

She hit send. This was about the tenth time that she'd texted Amanda. She still hadn't gotten any responses; part of her wondered if there was a chance that she'd written the phone number down incorrectly and was harassing some poor stranger. She decided not to worry about it too much, though; it wasn't like she expected Amanda to respond. At least not right away.

Next, Morgan typed a message to Luke. "Just to be one hundred percent sure – the dress code for tomorrow is like a cocktail party, right? You're sure that I don't need to have some sort of long gown?"

He responded almost instantly. "I was just going to text you actually. I'm really not feeling well – I'm so sorry, but I don't know that I can make it tomorrow."

What!

Almost every day for the past week, Luke texted her with some sort of teaser for this party – saying there'd be caviar appetizers, joking (or she thought he was joking?) about an elephant being there, and even saying that he was going to pick her up in a Ferrari. And now he was just going to up and cancel like it was nothing?

No – she *needed* to go to this party. This was her only chance to get more information about her mom's death. She responded right away.

"Luke! I bought an extremely fancy dress for this event." She paused – it wasn't really expensive, but he didn't need to know that. "If you back out on me now, after you built this up so much, I don't know that I can ever speak to you again."

She smiled to herself as she hit send. It wasn't true, of course – they had to work together at the very least – but it was hyperbolic enough that it might scare him.

Morgan slipped back into the second dress she'd gotten. It was black and more subtle than the red; it looked great with the chunky pearl necklace Jade gave her for her birthday. This dress seemed like it would help her blend into the crowd more. The last thing she needed was for Brock to recognize her and kick her out of his mansion. If only it were a masquerade ball or something...

Morgan's phone buzzed – it was Luke. "An extremely fancy dress? You're right – we can't allow that to go to waste. What am I thinking? I'll be there to pick you up in a horse and carriage, as promised."

"I thought it was a Ferrari?" she responded.

All he sent back was a winking face.

The next day, Morgan had one engagement photo shoot on the mainland but made sure that she got back to San Juan with plenty of time to shower, do her hair and makeup, and get into her black dress. Initially she planned to wear some impressively high heels to the party, but she realized that if she ended up having to run away and disappear into the woods, the shoes might hinder her escape.

So instead, she settled on a pair of sparkling rose gold wedges. They were an old favorite, very broken in, and good for a brisk jog in case anyone ended up threatening her with a weapon. In the worst case scenario, she could whip them off and throw them at an assailant. Her dad liked to complain that these shoes were basically "wooden blocks," and he wasn't completely wrong; she just planned to use that to her advantage.

At seven o'clock, Luke pulled into the driveway. Morgan and Jade, hiding in the living room, looked at each other and started giggling when they saw him. Jade offered to open the door for him, but Morgan told her to wait.

"I want to see if he's going to come up to the door or if he's going to sit in the car and honk at me, like an animal."

Luckily, Luke got out of the car and knocked on the door – almost like a gentleman. He even brought a bouquet of flowers, which for some reason made her feel embarrassed in front of Jade.

Jade, however, was unfazed. "Give those to me, I'll find a vase. You two kids go and have some fun!"

Morgan laughed. "Thanks Jade."

Once the front door was closed behind them, Luke stopped in front of her. "You look stunning. Whatever you paid for this very fancy dress was worth it."

"Thanks." She studied him for a moment. It seemed that he decided to go for a more casual outfit – he had a nice navy blue suit, but he didn't have a tie. His white shirt was unbuttoned, exposing a bit of his chest. It was so very *him* and so very perfect.

"You look okay too, I guess."

Luke laughed. "I knew that if I fished for compliments long enough you would give me one."

Morgan was going to make a sarcastic response but stopped dead in her tracks when she saw what was parked in the driveway. "What is *that*?"

"Ah yes. I'm sorry, but the romantic carriage that I ordered fell off the ferry on the way here. It was very tragic, it sank to the bottom of the Salish Sea."

"Are the horses okay?"

"Oh yes, they were powerful swimmers. They have the night off, grazing in their meadows, I imagine."

"Good." Morgan got a bit closer to the car – it was an Audi, but that was all she knew about it. She wasn't *actually* into cars. Was he trying to impress her?

"Is this yours?"

"Can we ever truly *own* anything?"

Morgan smiled. "What happened to your *other* car?"

"I couldn't very well drive my rusted piece of junk to a party with a bunch of car snobs," Luke said. "If you like, we can just take it joyriding for the rest of the evening. I'll take you anywhere you want to go."

"Tempting, but like I said – this dress can't be wasted."

"Of course, the dress." He walked to the passenger side to open the door for her. "After you Miss Allen."

"Thank you." Morgan slid into the cool leather seat. The car even smelled nice. "Did you steal this car? I feel like I have a right to know if I'm an accessory to grand theft auto."

Luke hopped into his seat. " 'Steal' is such an ugly word. I like to say 'borrow.' "

"Luke!" she turned to him. "Who did you steal this from?"

Luke started the engine. "Again, I *borrowed* this from my roommate Brad. Did he give me permission? No. Will he know that I took it? Perhaps. Will he be able to get to me? No, because I have his car."

"Ah, you're right. The perfect plan." She buckled her seat belt. "Are you feeling better? You don't seem sick at all."

Luke shrugged. "It's been a bit rough, to be honest. So again, if you'd like to go anywhere else –"

"Nope. Take me to the fancy party please."

He nodded before putting the car into reverse. "If you insist."

Luke took the long way to the other side of the island, insisting on a scenic view. Morgan didn't care about the view – she got to see it all the time. What she cared about was getting to that party as soon as possible and somehow distracting Luke so she could snoop without his questioning. The closer they got to the house, though, the more nervous she grew. She was sure that her forehead would be glistening with sweat by the time they got there.

When they pulled up to the house, a valet took the keys to the car.

"See? I couldn't show up here with my trash heap," Luke said under his breath.

Outside, Brock had several of his cars on display. People were slowly milling about, chatting and laughing and admiring the cars. Morgan paused, studying the scene to see if anything matched the description from the night that her mom died.

"Do you want to go and check those out?" asked Luke.

Morgan shook her head. "Maybe later – are those all the cars he has?"

"Uh, I'm not sure – maybe."

"I'd really like to see some of the more rare cars." Rare cars? Was that even how people talked about cars?

Luke squinted, then let out a sigh. "How about we go inside? And maybe later we can see something else."

Something else? What was he talking about? Was he onto her? Had Brock set her up? Although it seemed like a very elaborate set up for Brock to lure her here. What would he even want with her? To scare her? She wouldn't be scared!

Okay – none of that really made sense. She was just being paranoid.

"Sure, let's go."

They walked inside the mansion and were immediately handed glasses of champagne. Morgan took in everything around her – there were enough people here that she could disappear into the crowd, but not so many that Brock wouldn't see her. She needed to be careful.

"So who do you know here?" asked Morgan. She had to find someone that she could stick Luke with – just for bit – so she could go and explore the rest of the house on her own.

Luke waved a hand. "Oh you know – everyone. And no one."

At that exact moment, a woman with bleach blonde hair approached them. "Luke? Is that you?"

"The one and only."

She clapped her hands excitedly. "This is amazing! Did Brock hire you to make lattes or something?"

Before she could stop herself, Morgan groaned. Both the woman and Luke turned to look at her.

"Oh, I'm so sorry."

What she wanted to say was, "Do you really think people only exist to serve you?"

But instead she said, "These shoes are already killing me!"

The woman looked down and shook her head. "Oh, that's what you'll get with cheap shoes."

"Is it?" Morgan replied.

She felt Luke's hand on her elbow and realized that she was in great danger of failing her mission before it even started.

"Don't I know it!" she said in a light and airy tone.

The woman and Luke laughed. Good. Now if only this lady would go away. Or maybe she'd keep Luke for like, half an hour. That'd be great.

"I won't be making any coffee today Lorraine, but perhaps if you stop by and see me later this week?"

She brushed a hand across his chest. "Don't tempt me!"

Ew.

Morgan grabbed Luke by the hand. "Oh look over there!"

"What is it?" He said before realizing his error. "Oh! Right! Pardon us."

"Of course."

Morgan wove through the crowd, ignoring the ice sculptures, the trays of hors d'oeuvres, and the string orchestra playing classical music.

"That was interesting," said Luke when she finally stopped by the staircase. "You almost started a fight with the first person that you met. I believe that's a new record for you."

Morgan rolled her eyes. "*She* started it by being rude."

"Of course she's rude! She's a rich socialite who has nothing better to do than practice her thinly veiled insults."

Morgan frowned. She didn't really care about that woman – she didn't care about any of these people. But it didn't seem likely that she was going to survive very long at this party. She needed to get moving.

"Don't you know anybody else here? Maybe someone nice?"

"No – I don't think so." He looked up for a moment. "Yeah, not really. No."

She sighed. "Well if we have no one to talk to – maybe we should take the liberty to explore?"

"I don't think that's a good idea, what if –"

Morgan looked over her shoulder. "Oh come on, where's your sense of adventure? What do you think is up there?"

Luke put a hand out as if to stop her, but she was already darting up the stairs.

"Morgan!" he called out in a hoarse whisper.

She turned around and gave him a mischievous smile before finishing her ascent. If there was an office in this huge place, it was probably upstairs. And any evidence that he didn't want guests to see would surely be hidden away from the party. Maybe in his bedroom? Morgan wouldn't stop until she found something.

The upstairs seemed completely deserted! She debated which door to open first before going for the third on the left.

Dang – just a bathroom. She closed the door and went down the hallway to peak into another room. Bingo – this was a bedroom – possibly the master bedroom, but it was hard to tell because everything in this house was so big and unnecessarily grand.

She slipped into the room and closed the door behind her. Unfortunately, Luke followed her in.

"What are you doing?" he said in a low voice. "We can't be up here."

Morgan shrugged. "Why not? We're guests in this home, just like that snobby lady downstairs."

"Morgan, I'm serious. We have to leave right now."

She smiled. "Or what?"

"Or you could corrupt evidence in your mother's death."

Morgan stopped. *What* did he just say?

Chapter 21

Luke froze. Perhaps it wasn't the best idea to say that to her – but he needed to snap her out of it! He'd never seen her like this before, it was as though she was spiraling into madness.

"What do you know about my mom?"

"Not much," he whispered. "Because you didn't tell me anything. Matthew told me, and –"

Morgan crossed her arms and turned around. "*Matthew...*"

"I'm glad he did," Luke continued. "I had no idea that you had ulterior motives in coming to this party."

Morgan spun around. "How do I know that *you* didn't have ulterior motives in bringing me here?"

"What?"

That made no sense. As Luke was trying to work it out, the door to the bedroom flew open. Brock stood in the threshold, glaring.

"Oh, hey, hello!" Luke said as he got behind Morgan and started gently pushing her out of the room. "One of your guests got lost here, I was just –"

"Luke, cut the crap," Brock said. "What are you doing up here? Are you stealing more camera equipment?"

Luke let out an exaggerated laugh. "No no – of course not. It's a total misunderstanding –"

Morgan broke free of Luke's grasp. "I would say that he's more in the market for a car."

Luke tried to give her a stern look, but her stare at Brock was unbroken.

"That wouldn't surprise me at all," Brock said. "Seriously, what's the matter with you? Get out."

"Nothing at all is the matter, we're very sorry, and we'll be going now." Luke continued the futile effort to move Morgan, who seemed to have dug her heels into the carpeting.

"How do you guys know each other?" asked Morgan.

Brock rolled his eyes and looked at Luke. "I'm not going to ask you again, get your drunk friend out of here."

Luke finally made some headway, but as he got Morgan to the doorway, she started talking again.

"Do you think that Luke is just someone who exists to serve you coffee?"

Brock turned around, scowling. "I would never step foot in that disgusting coffee shop."

"Yes that is quite true, we really should be going," Luke said.

Morgan dropped her voice. "Then how *do* you know him?"

"He's sort of an old family friend," Luke replied in a low voice.

"Yeah, also known as an uncle." Brock called out behind them. "Close the door! Don't let me catch you up here again."

Luke shut the door and motioned for Morgan to follow him down the stairs. She stood there, arms crossed.

"Is that true Luke?"

He sighed. "Is what true?"

"That he's family?"

Luke frowned. "Well I've never really thought of him as family, exactly, but –"

"Is he or isn't he?"

Luke rubbed his eyes. If he said the wrong thing, she might turn around and burst through Brock's bedroom door again.

"Technically yes, he is my mother's brother. She passed away when I was little, though, and I only barely know him, and –"

"You're unbelievable."

Morgan took off down the stairs, her hair bobbing with each step. Luke didn't catch up to her until they got to the bottom of the staircase.

"How could you hide this from me?" she said, her voice rising.

Luke held up a finger. "I'll explain everything, but not in the middle of this party. You kind of have a bad history at parties."

Morgan was silent for a moment, appearing to consider what he was saying. "Fine."

She found her way through the crowd and into the backyard. There were still some guests close to the house, though, so she kept walking. Luke followed her until they were almost at the water's edge.

"I can explain everything," he said. "Last night, Matthew told me about how you were trying to get information out of him, which led him to tell me about your mom's case."

"Okay."

"So you see, I tried everything that I could to get you to not come here tonight. But you insisted, and then you started snooping around –"

"I was not snooping!"

"Then what do you call what you were doing?"

"Investigating. Luke, if you talked to Matthew, then you knew that Brock is definitely involved in my mom's murder."

Luke flinched at the word murder. It was such a *final* word – it didn't seem like it fit at a party like this.

Morgan narrowed her eyes. "What? You don't believe that someone from your family could do something like that?

Because he has expensive cars and a mansion and *ridiculous* white carpets?"

"Hey, just because he's rich doesn't mean he's a bad person."

"Right. Of course you'd say that. You're a rich kid, aren't you?"

"No. I mean – my family is comfortable, but –"

Morgan scoffed. "That's such a rich kid thing to say. From the moment I met you, you showed me who you really were. Rich or comfortable – whatever you want to call it – you don't ever think about other people."

"Now hold on –"

"No *you* hold on! Did you know that your uncle was able to get out of a DUI the night that my mom was murdered? Do you know why, Luke? Do you have any guesses?"

"That's not fair Morgan."

"What's not fair is that someone *murdered* my mother and he knows who did it, and there is *nothing* that I can do about it! But what do you care? You've got a pile of money waiting for you back home when you decide to stop driving around looking for yourself. Until then, you can just keep leaving people behind. That's what you do best, isn't it?"

"Maybe it is. But at least I'm not coming back to the same place again and again, looking for answers that don't exist."

Morgan's face fell and she said nothing. She turned and walked towards the direction of the forest.

"Oh come on! What are you going to do, walk all the way home?"

Morgan didn't answer or look back. Within a moment, she disappeared into the trees.

Chapter 22

It was a good thing that she wore wedges instead of heels – the wedges were much sturdier in the soft mud of the forest. Heels would've sunken into the muddy spots and slowed her down, and Morgan needed to move quickly so that she could get away from the house.

Looking for answers that don't exist.

He talked to Mathew *one* time and suddenly he's an expert on her mom's case? How did *he* know that the answers didn't exist – was it because Brock destroyed the evidence? Was Luke helping him cover it up?

She should have trusted her gut. She should have kept him at a distance and never let her guard down. At first, she could only guess that the bad feeling she had about Luke was because he was a jerk – a guy who thought he was so cool that he could get any girl he wanted.

Well not this girl!

But how was she supposed to know that he was not only faking who he was – this earnest guy, traveling around the country – but he was actually related to Brock? Maybe even a spy for Brock?

It was unreal. She had an inkling that they were in cahoots, but she didn't trust herself and thought she was being crazy. But she was right all along!

Morgan walked on Cattle Point Road for twenty minutes until she felt like she'd blown off some steam. Maybe she didn't have the most measured response to Luke, but at least she didn't cause a scene at the party. For most people that wouldn't be considered a success, but for Morgan it was something; next time she was in crisis, maybe she'd be able to completely hold her temper. Baby steps.

An ache in her knee caused her to stop walking. She couldn't walk all the way home, and she didn't want Luke to show up and try to argue with her more. She wanted to be away from him, and she didn't want him feeding any more information to Brock. The image of him doing that sent a chill down her spine.

She knew that she had to call someone and ask for a ride, but there weren't a lot of options. Ideally she would've asked Margie; Margie was nonjudgmental and probably wouldn't even ask questions if she got the vibe that things had gone poorly. But Margie had a lot going on – she didn't need this added to her plate.

Morgan stopped and pulled her phone out of the tiny purse she'd brought to match her dress. She had a text message – was it Luke?

No – it was Amanda, of all people. She actually answered!

"How's the party? I spent all weekend working."

Morgan scrunched her nose. Well, working the weekend seemed like a mistake – no wonder Amanda was so grumpy all the time. Morgan looked around to make sure that no cars were coming to run her over. The coast was clear. Everything was clear, actually – she had a beautiful view of Mount Finlayson and the shimmering waters in the moonlight.

She didn't know how to answer Amanda. On the one hand, Morgan felt sorry for herself, even though she knew it was a bit pathetic. But while she felt confused and hurt and betrayed, stopping to look at this beautiful scene made her feel small.

So small – but in a good way. It made her problems seem petite and manageable; they were nothing compared to the vast openness and possibilities of the ocean. And the wind whispering through the grasses quieted the panic in her mind; the gentle slopes of the hills promised peace and grace.

Morgan took two pictures – one of herself, not smiling, and one of the breathtaking view. "It was not great. Got in a fight with my date – long story – and now I'm trying to walk home, but it's a bit far in this outfit."

As comfortable as her shoes were, she couldn't walk ten miles in them. Morgan decided to take a seat in the grass and weigh her options. A moment later, Amanda's response came through. "Oh my gosh! That's terrible."

Shoot. Maybe she shouldn't have told her that; Morgan wasn't trying to encourage Amanda to keep working all the time and being miserable. "It's okay. Now I'm deciding whether to bother Margie to pick me up or to bother Jade to pick me up. Or if I want to hitchhike with a possible murderer. I've done it before, it was okay."

Morgan chuckled to herself. Why was she always stuck walking up and down this road? She needed to invest in a bicycle.

A message from Amanda popped up. "I think Margie or Jade are your best options."

Morgan smiled – at least she thought they were better than strangers. That was progress. Slow, but progress.

Morgan let out a big sigh before calling Jade. She picked up after a few rings.

"Hey! What's up?"

"Hey Jade. I wanted to see if you could – uh – come and pick me up."

"Oh no! What happened?"

"I got in a fight with Luke and..."

Morgan could hear Jade rustling around and getting her car keys.

"I'll be right there." Jade said. "Wait – where are you? Where is this party?"

"I started walking so I'm on Cattle Point Road, if you could just swing by there. You'll see me – the idiot in the black dress."

"You're not an idiot. I'm on my way."

Morgan stayed where she was, sitting on the grass. She was not looking forward to explaining the entire situation to Jade, who would inevitably take Luke's side, for no good reason, and tell her that she was being harsh. But Jade didn't understand – just as she didn't understand Amanda.

Yes, Amanda was being a brat, but Morgan knew the feeling – she was just lashing out. She was so engulfed by the grief of losing her mom that she didn't know what to do with herself. It seemed like she was working all the time so she could avoid facing the grief.

Morgan knew the feeling well because the grief swallowed her, too. She took a different approach, though. She decided to funnel all of her energy into being completely obsessed with finding her mom's murderer. From the outside it might look crazy or unhealthy, but to Morgan, it was how she was surviving.

When she saw Jade's car coming down the road, Morgan stood up and waved. For a moment, she weighed the option of not telling Jade the full story so she wouldn't get a lecture.

But no – she couldn't lie to Jade. Especially for the silly reason of being too afraid to face what she had to say.

"Hey," she said weakly as she got into the car.

Jade unbuckled her seat belt to reach across and hug her. "Are you okay? What happened?"

"Well..." Morgan looked into Jade's eyes for a brief moment before bursting into tears. It was always hard when someone used their nice voice to ask if she was okay.

"Oh my gosh, Morgan! I'm so sorry. I'm going to pull off the road so we can talk."

Jade turned and parked on a lookout viewing point. Morgan was still sniffling when they stopped, but she had herself under a bit better control.

"I'm sorry," Morgan said. "I've just been randomly bursting into tears recently. I don't know what's gotten into me."

Jade fished a packet of tissues from the back of the car. "You don't need to apologize. And you don't have to tell me what happened if you don't want to."

Typical Jade, killing her with kindness.

Morgan let out a breath, trying to steady herself. "No. I want to tell you. Even though I already know what you're going to say."

Jade laughed. "Am I that predictable?"

"No," Morgan shook her head. "It's just...you know."

She wiped the tears off of her face and blew her nose before diving into the story. She started from Luke asking her to go to the party, including the kayaking trip.

When Morgan finished with her argument with Luke, Jade sat quietly for a moment.

"What?" Morgan finally said, breaking the silence.

Jade frowned. "I'm just thinking. Trying to process everything that you said."

"You're not going to yell at me right away?"

"No. It's really not that simple."

Morgan blew her nose again. She managed not to cry, but there were a few moments where it was close. "You don't think so? And that everything's my fault?"

Jade shifted in her seat. "I mean, some of the things that you did were less than ideal. You said you were having doubts about Luke, right?"

"Yeah. And I was right!"

"Well – from what it sounds like, he only learned about your mom's case the night before the party. So I don't think that he had some grand scheme to trap you."

Morgan frowned. "Yeah, I guess that's technically right."

"So yeah, maybe he should've told you that Brock was his uncle. But also, you probably shouldn't have used him to get into that party."

Morgan groaned. "I *know*."

"It's understandable, you're really frustrated, and I get it. But..."

"But what?"

"Don't scream at me if I say this. Promise?"

"Yeah," Morgan said. She probably deserved whatever it was. "I promise."

Jade nodded. "Are you sure that finding your mom's killer will make you feel *that* much better?"

Morgan leaned back, thinking. "Honestly, I don't know. But it feels like the most important thing I can do, you know?"

Jade nodded. "I don't know, but yeah, I can understand that."

"I just feel so jumbled right now. I can't think straight, and whenever I think about my mom I feel like I'm going to cry again."

Jade turned the car on. "How about we go back home and you can sort out your thoughts and get some sleep?"

"What am I going to do about Luke?"

"Well," said Jade. "I don't think there's an easy answer to that. Do you like him?"

Morgan sighed. "Yes? No? I don't know. What he said was...so mean. And I don't like that he lied to me."

"Don't forget that you lied to him, too."

Morgan buried her face in her hands. "My life is a mess."

Jade laughed. "Oh please. Everyone's life is a mess! Look at my mom. Look at me! You're at least in good company. Let's go home, put a movie on, and get some sleep. You should give yourself a few days to think through this. It'll be okay."

Morgan turned to her and smiled. "Somehow I believe you."

Chapter 23

Luke considered going after Morgan, but what was the point? She clearly made up her mind about him from the moment they met; she only waited to collect more evidence to support her theory. She was no different than the countless people that he knew back home who made assumptions about him because of his father.

Only this time it wasn't just his father – it was his uncle, too. A person he didn't even particularly like! It wasn't his fault that he was related to these crappy men or that his family had money. He didn't have any money and he was sick of having to apologize for it. If Morgan thought his only plans in life were to go home and claim an inheritance, then she could go on thinking that. He didn't need to waste his energy to prove her wrong.

Luke walked back to the house and helped himself to some lobster and canapés before getting his – Brad's – car from the valet. He half expected to see Morgan trekking along the side of the road, but oddly, she was nowhere to be seen. She must've gotten someone to pick her up.

Good. He didn't want to drive her. She had this whole theory that he was traveling the US "looking" for himself, but that wasn't true at all. He was traveling the US to get *away* from all of the expectations on him – from his father, from his family, even from his friends and peers back home. And as soon as she learned a little bit about him, she behaved the same way everyone else did.

And why should he stick around the same place forever? Just so everyone could end up being disappointing? He thought she was different. He was willing to stay on this island for her, but not anymore.

Luke pulled into his driveway and shut off the car. Who was he trying to fool? Even on the other side of the world he couldn't get away from what people expected of him.

Nor could he get away from his family. He was guilty by association of his uncle's terrible acts. Who knew what Brock did on the night that Morgan's mom died?

Luke would certainly never be able to get it out of him. The man had million dollar lawyers to cover his every move. Brock probably drove drunk *all the time.* The man had no consideration for anyone. He only cared about himself and was almost a caricature of a rich jerk.

And that's what Morgan thought of Luke, too. Just another rich, selfish jerk.

He needed to keep moving. This would be his last night on San Juan Island.

He walked into the house where Brad was waiting for him.

"Seriously dude? You couldn't even *ask* to borrow my car?"

Oh. Right. It felt like a week ago that he took the car, but it'd only been a few hours. "Would you have said yes?"

Brad frowned. "Probably not."

"Yeah, I'm sorry. And you're right, I decided to just take it and make it up to you later."

Brad shook his head. "Alright, so how are you going to make it up to me then?"

"I'm not sure. I think I'll be leaving the island for a while – tomorrow. But you can have anything that you want."

Brad raised an eyebrow. "Anything?"

"Sure."

Brad thought for a moment. "Okay, if you're leaving, then give me your Xbox."

Luke laughed. "It's yours."

That was easy. All of the guys were constantly "borrowing" Brad's car. It was actually hilarious how often Brad went to grab his keys and someone else's keys would be in their spot. He was a nice guy – too nice to be pining after random girls on the island. If only Brad could learn to walk away.

Luke went upstairs and started to pack his things. All of the furniture came with the apartment, so it was nice that he wouldn't have to deal with selling it. He'd cover his rent until a new roommate was found, of course. After weighing his options, he decided to do a few loads of laundry that night – it would be harder to access a laundromat for the next week at least.

He wasn't sure exactly where he wanted to end up, but he knew that he wanted to go north. He wanted to explore Canada, and the summer would be a good time to start. He spent the rest of the night packing and went to bed around three in the morning. His plan was to catch the mid-afternoon ferry – it was important to have a good night's sleep before a day full of driving.

Luke wasn't sure what to tell Morgan – they had some weddings booked, but he could probably get one of the other videographers to cover. As soon as he woke up the next morning, he called one of the newer videographers he knew living on the mainland; they'd met a few weeks ago and he seemed eager to do shoots. Luke talked to him on the phone for about thirty minutes, explaining some of the upcoming gigs and checking if he was free.

He was – Luke told him that he'd send him some of the details later after he talked to Morgan. He'd keep it professional – just let her know that he was heading out of town and that he would make sure the weddings were covered. The brides wouldn't even know the difference – except for Jillian, of course. But who cared about Jillian?

When it was time to leave, he called his roommates into the living room and said goodbye. They all thought he was joking at first, but then they weren't quite sure. Why didn't people ever take him seriously?

It was strange leaving abruptly, sure, but otherwise it would get too drawn out. There would be a going away party, people might get him gifts. Then he'd feel guilty about wanting to throw the gifts away because they wouldn't fit in his car, and he'd throw them away anyway.

It was better this way. He said goodbye, got into his car, and drove to the ferry terminal. He was actually a bit early and got a spot at the front of the line. He turned off the car and walked over to the coffee shop by the ferry landing.

Oh shoot – he'd forgotten to say goodbye to everyone at Oyster Coffee. But who would even be working? He didn't have enough time to get over there and back to his car before the ferry left.

Oh well. Best not to risk it. He could video call them from his next stop. It didn't matter. People liked to make a big deal about him leaving, but really their lives would go on like nothing had happened. No one was going to miss him – not really.

He got a cup of coffee and went back to his car, sitting on the hood and looking out onto the water. He always loved this part of the island – the hustle and bustle of ferries and boats coming in and out, tourists and locals intermixing. He loved how the boats coming into the docks never looked like they were in a hurry – boats always looked like they were going *just* the right speed.

The freshness just off the water – he was going to miss that, too. He took a deep breath, savoring it. Maybe the next place he'd go would be by the ocean? He wasn't sure yet. He didn't know how far his money would take him.

The announcement to board the ferry rang out and Luke hopped back into his car. He turned the key in the ignition to no response.

"Oh come on," he grumbled. "Don't do this to me now."

He tried and tried, but nothing worked. The car wouldn't start, and the honks behind him rang out. He knew that he should've gotten a new battery – *why* hadn't he gotten that battery?

He opened the car door to yell to the attendant. "I seem to be stuck, do you think you could offer a jump?"

The guy, his belly popping out of the yellow safety vest, squinted at him and waved his arm. "Let's go!"

"My car won't start, is there any way –"

He shook his head and continued directing cars onto the ferry, motioning for the drivers to go around Luke. Finally, once all of the cars were onboard, the man approached Luke's window.

"Listen buddy, we can't make everyone wait for you. You're going to have to catch the next ferry."

"But isn't there anything –"

The man turned and walked away.

Great.

Luke sat back in his seat and groaned. He now had to call one of his roommates to come and pick him up after he so unceremoniously left for good? Talk about awkward.

Luke got out of the car and leaned against the door, rubbing his eyes. This wasn't a great start to his new adventure.

"Luke! Luke, hi!"

He looked up and squinted to see who was trying to get his attention. Walking rapidly towards him was a petite blonde woman and Uncle Brock.

"Hey," he called out. He didn't quite recognize the woman. Perhaps Brock's new flavor of the month?

"Oh my gosh, I can't believe that we ran into you like this," the woman said as she stretched up to give Luke a hug.

Luke shot Brock a puzzled look over her shoulder. "I know, how funny is that? This place is like a big little town."

She pulled away. "Really?"

"No, it isn't," said Brock with a stiff smile.

How exciting. Brock was pretending to be nice again. He only did that around women that he liked. This could prove to be useful...

"I'm so glad that you made it to the island," said Luke. "Forgive me, I know we've met but –"

"I'm Andrea. Andrea Collins, it's nice to finally meet you in person."

"That's right!" said Luke with a grin. "I've only seen you on a tiny screen. How perfect is this, the battery *just* died in my car!"

"Oh no!" she said. "Do you need a ride? Brockie just picked me up from Seattle in his yacht, and we stopped here for lunch."

Of course, the yacht. How could Luke forget? Probably because he never even got to take advantage of it. Morgan wouldn't believe that, of course.

"How lovely," Luke said with a smile. "Are you heading back now?"

Brock shifted his weight. "I'm leaving the ship here for a tune up. My driver is coming to get us."

"Oh, perfect," Luke said. "I was hoping you'd offer me a ride Uncle."

"Of course," Brock replied.

"I'm making friends already," squealed Andrea.

Luke resisted the urge to cover his ears. "So, remind me, is this your first time on the island?"

Her smile faded. "Uh – kind of. Yes. It is, it's the first time."

Weird answer, but Luke wasn't one to judge. "How nice! How long are you staying? Do you plan to do any hiking or kayaking?"

She shook her head. "I don't think that's a good idea. I'm sticking to Brock's place, mostly."

"There's some really lovely kayaking and biking though, I have a few friends –"

"No," Brock said firmly. "We're not interested."

Luke smiled and nodded, but he didn't get what the big deal was. Did the woman not know how to ride a bike? She did look like someone who would melt if any water splashed on her, but that was true of all of Brock's lady friends.

He dropped the subject and Brock's driver arrived. They piled into the back of the car; Luke amused himself by wedging between them.

"Don't you think you'd be more comfortable up front?" asked Brock.

"And miss any time with this enchanting lady?" said Luke. "Never."

She smiled widely. "You're even *more* charming in person."

Luke was only able to suppress his laugh because of the look of death that his uncle shot him. "Oh stop."

"I'm so glad not to be driving," continued Andrea.

"Darling," Brock said, "I think you've had too much champagne."

"What?" She hiccuped. "We both know that I can't drive on this island."

Luke looked up, catching another of Brock's death stares – but this time it was directed at Andrea.

"Oh come on," she said with a groan. "He's family. It's fine."

Brock ignored her. "Why don't you tell us about where you were going, Luke?"

Luke felt like a block of ice slipped down the back of his shirt. "Oh, me? I was just going to the mainland to see a friend. It looks like it'll have to be postponed for now."

Chapter 24

That Saturday, Jade was on her own. Morgan had a wedding to shoot, and luckily, Luke wasn't involved – a friend of the groom was doing the videography for that particular wedding. Jade thought it was for the best, because Morgan still seemed quite confused about him. She let Morgan know that she was available if she needed to talk, but didn't push the topic.

Jade made plans to hang out with her mom that evening. The plan was to pick up dinner in town, then they were going to bake cookies and rent a movie. It was a real girl's night, and Jade was looking forward to it. It had been ages since they had time for something like this.

She swung by their favorite sandwich shop to get dinner and decided to make a detour to grab a bottle of wine. After parking her car outside of the convenience store, she hopped out and rushed to the door – she didn't want to keep her mom waiting. Just as she reached the store, the door flung open and almost hit her in the head.

"Oh my gosh, I'm so sorry!"

Oh no. It was Matthew. "It's okay! You almost got me, but you didn't."

"You've got some pretty fast reflexes."

"You have to around here," she said with a smile. "Or you'll end up with a black eye."

He stepped aside to hold the door open for her. "After you."

"Thanks, I'm just running in to get a bottle of wine."

"Oh, got a hot date tonight?"

Jade spun around; she couldn't quite make out what he said. "I'm sorry?"

"Oh – I was just kidding, I asked if you had a hot date – not that you *couldn't* have a hot date, but..."

Ah, so she *hadn't* misheard him. "If you call my mom a hot date, then yes."

"I feel like either way I answer that would be inappropriate," he said with a laugh. "Do you mind if I come in with you?"

Jade shrugged. She couldn't very well say that she minded. "Do you have any wine recommendations?"

"I can't say that I do. I'm more of a beer guy myself."

Jade slowly made her way to the back. Was he going to say something about Brandon? She really hoped not. It'd be better if some things were left unsaid.

"I'm actually really glad that I ran into you," he said.

"Oh?"

"Yeah, I don't know if you saw but John Mulaney is doing a show in Seattle next weekend."

Jade forced herself to stare forward as though she were carefully studying every bottle of wine on the shelf. "Is he that comedian with the dimples?"

"Uh – maybe? Can't say I ever paid attention to his dimples."

Jade laughed. "I wouldn't expect you to."

"Well I have two tickets, the seats are pretty good, and was wondering if you'd want to go with me?"

Jade stopped, reached forward and took the bottle of wine directly in front of her. "It's really nice of you to offer, but I'm completely booked next weekend. Maybe another time?"

"Oh – sure. No problem."

She made her way to the register. "But I hope you have a good rest of your night."

"You too. Let me know if – if you need anything."

"Sure!"

Jade kept her eyes focused on the register, then on getting the money out of her wallet, and then on the receipt as it printed. She only cautioned a glance out of the window when she was sure that Matthew was back to his car.

For some reason, she found herself unable to look at him. She wasn't expecting to be ambushed like that at the convenience store! She was not expecting to see him, and she certainly didn't anticipate that he was going to ask her out!

She went outside and got into her car. Was he really asking her out, though? It sounded like he just had an extra ticket. It didn't seem like it was a big deal. If he hadn't run into her, he probably wouldn't even have asked her to go.

Great, and now she had to make sure that she stayed home next weekend so he wouldn't see that she didn't actually have any plans. But wait – if he was in Seattle, then he wouldn't know that she had lied, right?

Jade closed her eyes. What a mess this was.

Even if Matthew *was* asking her out, which she wasn't sure he was, it didn't matter. She would never say yes – she never could say yes. He was a nice guy – a really nice guy. He deserved to be with someone like him. He deserved to be happy.

Jade didn't know what she deserved, but it wasn't that. It seemed like Brandon's little stunt finally forced him to move along with the divorce, so that was good. She shouldn't have to keep fighting with him. But no – she didn't deserve a chance with a guy like Matthew. How could she even have thought he was asking her out?

Maybe she'd spend the rest of her life driving sandwiches over to her mom's house and renting romantic comedies. Her mom needed her. No – they needed each other.

As Jade made the drive to the other side of the island, she ran through everything in her mind. She was determined not to betray how she felt to her mom. They were going to have a nice night – her mom had been quite down about her breakup with Hank. She didn't need to deal with Jade's drama, too.

She let herself in when she got to the house and could hear that her mom was on the phone; she followed her voice to the kitchen.

"Oh hang on, Jade just got here." Her mom gave her a quick hug. "You want to talk to her? Oh, of course!"

Jade gave her a puzzled look as she accepted the phone. She mouthed, "Who is it?" and her mom whispered, "Amanda!"

Jade put the phone to her ear. "Hello?"

"Hey Jade. How are you doing?"

"I'm good, how are you?"

"I've been better." Amanda said with a sigh. "Look – I just talked to your mom and apologized for the way that I've been behaving. And I want to apologize to you too. You were both so nice when I came to visit and I was...awful. I'm so sorry, there's no excuse for it. I hope that someday you can forgive me."

What on *earth* was going on today? Was it a full moon? "Oh – it's okay. Really."

"Your mom is such a lovely person. Anyway – that's all I had to say. I'm just...sorry. I'll let you guys have your dinner. Have a good night!"

"You too!"

Jade set the phone down and stared at her mom. "What was *that* all about?"

"You won't believe it," she said, beaming. "Amanda's had a change of heart. It seemed like it came out of nowhere! She called with a very kind apology. I was shocked!"

"*I'm* shocked!"

"And she asked if it was too late to re-invite everyone to the wedding."

"Are you serious?"

She nodded. "Yes! She said that she wants us to be happy, that we both deserve to be happy, and that she's sorry, and she hopes that the wedding can go off without a hitch."

Jade leaned against the kitchen counter; she felt a bit dizzy. "Mom! This is amazing!"

"I know!"

Jade dropped the bag of sandwiches and wrapped her arms around her mom for a hug. "I wonder what made her change her mind."

"I do too."

"Do you think there's any chance that this is...like, temporary? She was so unpleasant before."

Her mom took a deep breath. "You know...grief is dark and mysterious. It takes a long time to find your way through it."

"So you think she's over it now?"

She smiled and shook her head. "I don't think you ever 'get over' grief. It chews you up and spits you out a different person. And then it follows you around, in a quieter way, forever."

Yikes. Jade didn't know what to say. She'd never really thought about it. After a moment, she cleared her throat. "I guess you're right. Are you going to call Chief Hank?"

"No – not right now. This is our night."

Jade pulled her cell phone out of her purse. "Oh come on Mom! If you don't call him, I will."

"Are you sure?"

"Of course! And I'll even give him some of my sandwich. But just a little bit. Maybe like a third of it."

Her mom went into the other room to make the call and Jade took a seat. She felt happy, but disoriented. She would need some time to herself after all of the events of today.

Chapter 25

When Luke called Brock on Sunday morning, he was surprised to hear Andrea answer.

"Hello!" she said in a singsong voice.

"Hi Andrea, how are you?"

"Oh it *is* you! I'm just lovely. How are you?"

"Quite good, thanks. I was hoping to speak to my uncle?"

"Unfortunately, he's still sleeping. *Someone* drank a bit too much last night."

"Ah, I see. When he wakes up – could you tell him that I have to talk to him about something important?"

"Oh," she cooed. "Sounds exciting! Why don't you come over for brunch today, around eleven? We're having a chef from Seattle prepare a four course brunch. You know, to get a good start to the week."

"That does sound like a good start to the week," replied Luke. "I would love to."

Brad allowed Luke to borrow his car on the condition that he would bring him lunch when he came back.

He went straight to Brock's house and arrived just before eleven. The front door was open and he let himself in. There were a lot of voices coming from the back rooms.

He called out a "Hello?"

"Luke! You're here!" squealed Andrea. "I'm so glad you could make it."

Luke peered into the dining room to see that there were about a dozen people chatting and drinking champagne.

"I'm so sorry, I'm afraid I'm a bit underdressed," he said.

"Nonsense," she said as she brushed a hand across his chest. "You look better than half of these people."

Luke returned her smile. "Is Uncle Brock awake?"

"There he is!" boomed Brock's voice.

Luke turned around to see that Brock was walking towards him, arms outstretched.

"Hello Uncle."

"My favorite nephew." Brock squeezed him tightly in a hug.

How much champagne did these people have?

"Listen, Uncle Brock – I need to talk to you about a little issue. And Andrea, it concerns you too."

"Oh, doesn't *this* sound serious?" Andrea said with a giggle.

Luke dropped his voice. "It's about the accident."

Both Brock and Andrea froze. Now he had their attention.

"Can we go somewhere private?" asked Luke. "I don't mean to scare you, but it's somewhat time sensitive."

Brock nodded. "Let's go upstairs to my office."

Andrea went up first, then Luke. Brock paused before he followed, turning around to make sure that no one was watching. When they got to the office, Brock locked the door.

"You better start talking and you better talk fast," said Brock.

"Alright, no need to get upset. I just stumbled into this. I have a friend who's a new deputy at the sheriff's department. He was given a cold case to look into."

"I have no idea what this has to do with me," said Andrea. The whimsical tone disappeared from her voice.

"He started telling me about the circumstances – and let me just say, I'd never heard of the accident. It was for some woman – Kelly Allen, I think? Who was hit by a car last year on the island."

"Lower your voice," Brock growled.

Luke cleared his throat. "Look – I'm trying to help you. He told me all of this information about this case, and he really shouldn't have. I know details that the public isn't supposed to know. And I think they're about to crack it wide open."

Andrea stood and rushed towards the door. "I need to get out of here."

Brock grasped her arm with surprising force. "Stop it. This is the kind of behavior that gets you in trouble in the first place."

"No need to be so rough, Uncle," Luke said soothingly. "I'm here to help."

Andrea took a seat on a nearby chair, rubbing her wrist.

Brock turned to Luke. "How do I know that you're not just working with the cops?"

Luke put his hands up. "I have nothing to gain, do I? The man joined my trivia team, I got this information, and I came here. And don't look so grave – this is a problem easily fixed. I already have a plan."

"This cop, he's your friend?" Andrea's voice shook. "But you're going to help me, right?"

"Of course I am!" Luke said.

Brock stopped pacing the room. "Why should we trust you?"

"You're right Uncle, I'm wearing a wire and recording this entire conversation."

Andrea giggled.

"Everything you say and do can be used against you in a court of law," Luke continued.

"What do they have?" asked Brock, his brow furrowed.

Luke took a deep breath. "A lot. Well, bits and pieces – enough now that they're going to arrest Andrea as soon as they realize that she's on the island."

Her eyes brightened. "But they don't know I'm here yet?"

Luke shook his head. "I don't think so. What they have – what I saw at least – was a video of you driving the Corvette."

Her jaw dropped. "They have a *video*?"

"I'm afraid so," Luke said with a nod. "I'm not sure if it was before or after you hit Kelly with the car."

Brock frowned. "Where was the video shot?"

"I'm not familiar enough with the roads on the island to say," Luke replied with a shrug. "The car didn't seem to be damaged, though. So for all they know, you were just out for a drive."

Andrea shook her head. "It wasn't *that* damaged after I hit her – not really. She kind of got stuck under one of the tires and I had to reverse. It was just a mess!"

"That's enough," said Brock sharply. "He doesn't need to know the details."

Luke nodded. "Right. But listen – I have a friend who runs a ferry service from Friday Harbor to Victoria."

"Canada?" Andrea groaned. "I mean, do I *have* to leave the country?"

"I can get you on the ferry today. Once you're out of the US, you can go wherever you like. But I don't think that you should ever return to the island."

Brock crossed his arms. "And I'm supposed to believe that you're doing all this out of the goodness of your heart?"

"Naturally, Uncle! Although...in order to safely transport your lovely friend out of the country, I will need to borrow a car."

"Of *course*," said Brock. "What's wrong with your car?"

"Like you saw, the battery is dead. And I may need to borrow this car for a few weeks, you know, staying away from this hot zone of activity."

Andrea stood up and grabbed Brock's hands. "You'll do it, won't you babe? I can pay for the car – it's no problem. I'll call Daddy and he'll have the money sent over immediately, no questions asked."

"You don't have to send the money, babe." Brock leaned in, resting his forehead on hers. "I can afford to lose another car. I can't afford to lose you."

They kissed deeply and it seemed like they'd never stop, so Luke interrupted them.

"Alright Bonnie and Clyde – we need to leave *now*. Andrea – don't bother grabbing your stuff, Brock can bring it later, okay?"

"Okay!" she squealed. "This is so exciting! I feel like I'm in a movie."

"Me too," said Luke.

After a brief haggle over which car Luke would be allowed to take, he ended up with the Volkswagen Golf GTI. Definitely one of the less showy cars, but Luke was happy with this upgrade to his situation.

Andrea hopped into the front seat with a large pink bag – apparently she ignored his directions not to pack anything.

"I just needed a few of the essentials," she said as she closed the door.

"Okay, just throw it in the back. You know – I think it might be best if you crouched down so that no one could see you driving through town."

She gasped. "Oh my gosh, that's a *really* good idea."

She tried to lean her seat all the way back but she was still visible from the window.

Luke shook his head. "I think you need to just lean forward and hug your knees."

"Okay!"

Luke started the car and waved goodbye to Brock.

"Now Andrea..."

"Yes?" she replied in a muffled voice.

"We're on quite the adventure together."

She giggled. "I know! I think I like going on adventures with you."

Luke cleared his throat and kept his eyes straight ahead. "And I you. I have to say, I didn't like how rough my uncle was back there."

"Oh – I was just being rash."

"Does he often grab you like that?"

Andrea was quiet for a moment. "I don't know."

"Did he do something to you the night of the accident?"

She sighed. "Well...he had too much to drink and was being mean. I saw something on his phone with another girl and we got into a fight."

"How awful," said Luke.

"And I just wanted to get away from him, and also, kind of get back at him. So I decided to take his precious Corvette."

"Had you been drinking?"

"Yeah, I totally wasn't myself."

Luke nodded. "I see. Well I can understand how it could get out of hand."

Andrea popped up to look at him. "And that stupid lady was just walking around in the dark!"

"Ah ah," Luke said, pushing her head back down. "We don't want anyone to see you."

"Oh right," she said, "Sorry. Anyway, I didn't see her until it was too late."

"That must have been *awful* for you."

"Oh it was *horrible*! Those old sports cars don't have a lot of clearance, you know? So she wasn't totally underneath – I don't know actually. I panicked and I had to get out of there. Luckily Brock came to his senses and helped me."

"Yeah, luckily. Okay listen – I need to make one stop so that we don't have any trouble with crossing the border. Keep your head down, okay?"

She turned to flash a smile at him. "Okay!"

Luke put the car into park and removed the keys. He *almost* felt bad about what he was doing – but actually no, he didn't.

He got out of the car where Chief Hank and Matthew were waiting.

"Hello gentlemen," Luke said as he approached them. "I trust that you were able to hear all of that?"

Chief Hank nodded. "We were."

"And did I satisfy the law with my statement that I was recording the conversation?"

Chief shrugged. "Maybe. We'll find out in court. But you did as well as could be expected."

Not exactly praise, but he didn't expect much from Chief. "Well here she is. I told her to keep hiding. I think it's kind of funny. We should leave her like that for a few hours."

Matthew laughed and shook his head. "Thanks Luke. You did great."

Luke nodded before taking a step back to remove himself from the action. It looked like the entirety of the sheriffs department was about to close in on the little black Volkswagen.

Good. It was about time.

Chapter 26

Morgan hadn't heard from Luke in over a week; she was starting to wonder if maybe he really *did* leave the island. She considered texting him, but clearly he was mad at her and she didn't know what to say. So instead of facing it like an adult, she scheduled her client meeting that Sunday at Oyster Coffee.

It was a lame attempt to see him and ultimately, a failure – he wasn't there. She considered asking the barista if she'd seen him around, but she felt too awkward to actually do it and didn't know what she'd do if the answer was "yes."

To top it all off, the couple that she met with said that they didn't want a videographer, so she lost *that* excuse to talk to him, too! They really only had a few more weddings to shoot together...unless he called those off entirely.

No, Luke wouldn't do that. Probably.

After the client meeting, she planned to go to Margie's to help with invitations. Ever since Amanda called off her embargo on the wedding, they were all hands on deck to get everything ready in time. Margie didn't want anything fancy, of course, but both Jade and Morgan wanted to make things special for her.

She was about halfway to Margie's when her phone rang. It was Chief Hank.

"Hey Chief!"

"Hey, where are you?"

"I'm driving to your fiancée's house to help plan your upcoming nuptials. You got the samples for that leopard print tuxedo we ordered, right?"

"Listen kiddo, I need you to pull over for a second. I've got some news."

Morgan frowned. "I'm not going to pull over, I'm going to see you in like five minutes. Just tell me then."

"I'm not at the house. Just find somewhere to stop."

Morgan rolled her eyes, but did as she was told. She pulled into a long driveway, hoping that the people inside the house wouldn't come out with a shotgun and tell her to buzz off.

"Alright, I stopped. What's up?"

"We have someone under arrest for the death of your mom."

Morgan's ear suddenly felt hot; she switched the phone to the other side. "What? Is this a joke?"

"No. This is not a joke."

Numbness spread throughout her body, almost like all of her limbs were falling asleep at once. "I can't believe this. How did you find them? Who is it?"

"It's a long story. Do you want to come down to the sheriff's office and we can talk?"

"Yes! I'll be right there."

Chief cleared his throat. "But you are *not* going to see, interrogate or harass the suspect, understand? This isn't a TV show."

"No no, I get it," she said as she put her car into reverse. "I promise I won't do anything crazy. I'll be there soon."

"See you."

She ended the call and was about to throw her phone into the backseat when she realized that she needed to call her dad. She put the car back into park – really hoping that these people weren't home – and dialed his number. Luckily he answered and she was able to tell him everything she knew; it wasn't much, but he was also excited.

"Okay Dad, I'm going to go to the sheriff's office right now and get more information. I'll call you as soon as I'm done and let you know what the next steps are, okay?"

"Okay! Love you sweetheart."

"Love you too."

Morgan took a few deep breaths after ending the call. She didn't need to get into a car accident on the way there and complicate things. Once she felt a little more stable, she slowly backed out of the driveway and drove towards Friday Harbor.

It felt like it was taking a lifetime to get into town. Everyone on the road kept nearly slowing to a halt to make turns. The woman ahead of her appeared to be driving ten miles an hour, unable to decide where she was supposed to go. After fourteen agonizing minutes, Morgan finally made it to the sheriff's department. She went straight to Chief's desk.

"That was fast," he said, looking up from his computer.

"Maybe for you. But I've been waiting for this news for over a year."

He smiled. "Fair enough. Okay, how about we go into a room so I can tell you what's going on."

"Sure."

She followed him into a small conference room. A large table took up most of the space, and it was surrounded by chairs which made it hard to even get by.

"I apologize that I don't have anything that's more welcoming," he said, motioning for her to take a seat. "Do you want a coffee?"

"No, I'm good, thanks. So what happened? Did you get more evidence?"

Chief took a seat across from her. "We did. Actually, Matthew played a big role in it."

Morgan tapped her finger on the table. "I always knew that I liked him."

Chief continued. "He's been looking at the evidence in the case since he started here."

"And he solved it?"

"Well – sort of. Kind of like you, he became fixated on the video. The one of the woman driving in the Corvette."

Morgan nodded. "Yeah, sure."

"We couldn't identify her, though, and we had no other evidence. He mentioned this to someone else, and *that* person made the connection."

"They knew the woman?"

Chief nodded. "He did. You know what – why don't you just talk to him so you can get the full story. Just go easy on him, okay?"

Morgan turned around to watch as Chief walked toward the door. "Why would I be mean to the person who solved my mom's murder?"

Chief didn't answer. He disappeared and returned a moment later, peeking his head into the room. "Hey kid?"

She stood up, straightening out her shirt. She wanted to look presentable to this person – before she jumped up and inappropriately hugged them. "Yes?"

He opened the door fully to reveal Luke standing behind him.

"Hi Morgan."

"Uh, hi Luke. I didn't know that you were still on the island."

He took a step into the room. "I am."

"Oh. What are you doing here?"

Chief cleared his throat. "Morgan – Luke was the one who broke the case. But I'll let him tell you about it."

Chief closed the door behind him, leaving them alone. It suddenly felt even stuffier than before. Morgan stood and stared at Luke, studying his outline against the peeling yellow paint of the walls.

"It was you?"

Luke held up a finger. "Yes, but before you yell at me – as soon as I realized that there might be a connection, I went and talked to Matthew. You can't accuse me of hiding this information, because I didn't know any of it."

Morgan continued staring.

"Do you want to take a seat?" he said. "You look quite pale."

Morgan nodded and sat down. "So...what happened?"

"Well this is rather embarrassing," Luke said with a sigh. "But after our fight..."

Morgan interrupted him. "I'm really sorry about that. I've been meaning to talk to you, but I didn't know how to. The things that I said were really out of line. And I'm sorry."

Luke smiled. "Actually, you weren't out of line. I hate to admit it, but you were right. And as soon as you said that about me – that I was just going to run away – that's exactly what I did. I tried to catch the ferry the next day to leave the island for good."

Morgan sat back and crossed her arms. "You were just going to leave without saying goodbye?"

"I know," he said, rubbing his face. "It was childish. I'm not going to make any excuses. I didn't know what else to do. I didn't know...how to face the truth."

Now she felt even worse; clearly her words had an effect on him. Morgan spent a lot of time gabbing, but she never *actually* expected people to listen to her. She wanted to reach across the table and hold his hand to comfort him, but decided against it.

"You really should learn not to take me too seriously."

He put up a hand. "No, you were right. Well, not about all of it actually – I'm not a spoiled rich kid like you think – but I don't know how to deal with my problems. So I run."

She sighed. "You're not a spoiled rich kid. And I get the urge to run."

"It's an easy way out," he said. "Anyway, as I was waiting to get on the ferry, my car battery died again."

Morgan bit her lip so she wouldn't smile. No need to be rude.

"And that's when I ran into my Uncle Brock. He'd just gotten back to the island with his girlfriend Andrea. Mind you, I had *never* met her before. I saw her on a video call once, but I didn't think anything of it. My uncle always has women coming and going."

Morgan raised an eyebrow. "Does he? Is that a family trait?"

"No. We are not at *all* alike," Luke said sternly. "We are related by blood but not much else. I avoid him unless...well, unless he can be useful. My camera, for example, is technically his camera."

Morgan smiled. "Ah, right. I know how you like to borrow things."

Luke smirked. "And basically, I made him give me a ride, and on the way, they both made some comments that struck me as odd. Nothing terribly obvious, but something was just... off. And I had your mom's case swirling in my mind, and I knew that at least he was involved in some way. But he's such a piece of work that I never expected he'd admit to anything. That's what I mean when I said – well, you know."

"I do," Morgan said with a nod.

"After that, I went to talk to Matthew and I convinced him to show me the video of the driver. It was Andrea – there's no doubt that it was her."

Morgan leaned forward. "And then what?"

Luke sat back. "It was tricky. They're both wealthy, both powerful. We came up with this crazy idea that I would convince them that I needed to smuggle Andrea off of the island – that the police were on her heels. And I recorded her confessing to what she did, too, but I had to tell her that I was recording because you can't legally record in Washington state unless both parties are aware. But both of them thought that I was joking, and she basically confessed to the whole thing. And then I drove her right to the police."

Morgan sat back. "Wow."

"I know," said Luke. "I didn't know if it was going to work, but we had no other options and no other evidence. She's the daughter of an oil tycoon, so she will have exceedingly good lawyers, and I'm really hoping that what we did isn't thrown out in court..."

Morgan reached across the table and grabbed his hand. "Thank you, Luke."

He looked down, then back at Morgan. "I wish I could do more."

"What you did was incredible. And I mean – what you said about me was right, too. I became obsessed with finding out who killed my mom. And when I knew that it was somehow connected to your rich uncle...I think deep down I knew that I would never get answers. And it drove me insane."

Luke squeezed her hand. "More insane than your baseline?"

"Yes," she said with a laugh. "The baseline is helpful for crashing parties and walking several miles in heels. But that *extra* level of crazy helps me break into people's homes."

Luke laughed. "I still can't believe that you did that."

"I know, me too, I can't believe it was such a waste. He called the police and Chief was there in no time. I couldn't even get into the garage."

"You're not a very good detective."

She shook her head. "I'm not."

Luke wrapped both of his hands around hers. "So now that it's over – well, now that it's *kind of* over, how do you feel?"

She paused for a moment to enjoy the warm comfort of his hands around hers. "I...I'm not sure, to be honest. I was really excited when I heard that Chief arrested someone, and I rushed over here. And now...I mean, I know it's going to be a long battle and everything. I'm glad that she's under arrest...but I wonder if Jade was right."

"About what?"

Morgan sighed, pulling away from him to cross her arms. "She asked if it would really make me feel better to catch my mom's killer. And I do feel better but...I don't know, it's hard to explain."

"That's okay," said Luke. "This is a lot to process. But I'm glad that I could be a part of it. I'm glad that I didn't run away."

"Me too."

He extended his hand back across the table. "You know Morgan..."

She smiled. "Yes Luke?"

"You're being rather selfish. You haven't asked once how I feel."

An involuntary snort-laugh escaped from Morgan's mouth. "I'm sorry Luke. How *do* you feel?"

"Finally." He stood up and walked around the table, taking a seat next to her. "My feelings for you have not changed. I understand that you've had some...reservations about me. But I can assure you, my focus all of this time has been entirely on you."

She felt like she'd lost her breath for a moment. "I know."

"I'm not sure what else I can do to prove my devotion."

Morgan smiled. "Do you have any other family members that we can get arrested?"

"I will gladly assist with anyone you choose," he said, leaning forward. "Just tell me who."

"That won't be necessary, at least not for now." Morgan leaned in. "I think I'm ready to take your word for it."

"I was hoping you'd say that."

Morgan inched towards him, taking in the smell of his cologne, before closing her eyes and pressing her lips against his.

He kissed her back before pulling away. "Hang on, does this mean that we're both going to run away, then?"

She shook her head. "No more running, Luke. We're in this together."

He pulled back a bit, studying her face. "I rather like the sound of that. Alright, you've convinced me."

Morgan smiled; if anyone was convinced, it was her. She leaned in and kissed him again.

Epilogue

On the morning of the wedding, Jade felt like a ball of nerves.

"Did you hear back from the caterer yet?" she asked Morgan.

"*No*! I knew that we should've gotten someone else. I don't know why we let Chief have a say in the food."

Jade sighed. "He said he wanted barbecue. And they were the only people who would do it."

Morgan threw her mascara into a duffel bag. "Yeah – never letting him make a decision again."

"I guess if there's no food, we can order a bunch of pizzas or something."

"No," groaned Morgan. "That's *not* going to work!"

"There's not much we can do now. Are you ready to go?"

Morgan stood for a moment, looking around before responding, "I guess."

When Jade opened the front door, Luke was just pulling into the driveway. He'd offered to drive them over and then help get things set up in the barn.

"Good morning!" he yelled out of the open window.

"Hey Luke!" Jade walked over and let herself into the back-seat of the car.

"Oh – sorry about that enormous platter," he said, turning around to drag the large container across the backseat. "I thought it would be nice to get a tray of breakfast sandwiches so everyone getting ready had something to eat. But I didn't expect them to make it half the size of my car."

Jade smiled as she buckled her seat belt. "That was very thoughtful of you Luke."

"I found that it's best to keep Morgan fed. When she gets hungry, she is more likely to climb on top of tables and verbally attack your entire family."

"Hey!" Morgan stood just outside of the car, arms crossed. "You shouldn't say things about me when I'm not around."

"What do you mean, I knew you were there all along. And I'm sorry, I was just telling Jade how dangerous it is to allow you to get hungry –"

Morgan leaned in and gave him a kiss on the cheek. "Alright, that's enough."

"Yeah," Jade added. "*Obviously* I know how much of a terror she is when she's hungry."

"Is today attack Morgan day?" She slid into the front seat of the car. "Because I thought it was Margie and Chief's wedding day and I'm already on my best behavior. A lot of these people have already seen me at my worst."

Jade laughed. "Don't worry, most of the people from my dad's party weren't invited to the wedding."

"Except," added Luke, "for Jade's father. You might remember him, because he is *also* your father."

Morgan groaned. "I am not going to talk to him, and I am not going to make a scene. I am going to be a perfect lady."

"It's going to be just fine," said Jade, even though she had a knot in her stomach. She was glad that her dad decided to come, though it did make things a bit awkward. Watching Morgan work herself into a tizzy over everything was an amusing distraction, though.

Predictably, when they got to the house, her mom was nowhere to be found; they eventually figured out that she was running around the barn, trying to do everything herself. Morgan ordered her to let go of the ladder she was clutching and hand it, along with all other wedding responsibilities, to Luke.

"Don't let him fool you," Morgan assured her. "He's more than just a pretty face."

"That's right," said Luke. "My face will not interfere with this task, dear bride. I will have everything running smoothly in no time."

Jade giggled to herself. They bantered back and forth like that all the time, and they could nearly always keep themselves from laughing. Morgan and Luke were quite the match – Jade had never seen Morgan so happy. And despite all of Morgan's previous concerns, Luke was proving to be a model boyfriend.

Jade was glad for them; Morgan deserved to be happy. And her mom deserved to be happy. Jade was still working out what she deserved, though.

After Brandon had that episode where he threatened her, his lawyer convinced him to finalize the divorce. It'd been official for a few months now, and Jade was still getting used to the feeling that she was finally free of him. On Morgan's recommendation, she started to see a counselor to work through her feelings about her marriage and the divorce.

The counselor tried to convince her that she deserved to be happy, too. She didn't quite believe it yet, but she was trying. There was a *little* excitement in her heart – Matthew was coming to the wedding. It would be nice to see him – he hadn't made it to the last few Sunday dinners.

They wrestled her mom away from the barn, leaving the remaining tasks in the capable hands of Luke, Connor, and

Jacob. Tiffany was already back at the house, anxiously waiting to get started on hair and makeup.

Her mom, of course, was unconcerned about how she looked. But it was their job to make sure that for once, she would get to feel pampered and adored.

They had fun getting ready, and towards the end, Amanda joined in, too. It was a little awkward at first, but Tiffany helped her put her hair up into an elegant twist, and after that, Amanda started talking a mile a minute. They were all abuzz with excitement when the car came to pick them up.

It seemed like the morning was flying by too quickly. Jade kept her cell phone with her to take pictures. They had a photographer along with them, of course – but she wanted some pictures of her own to savor the moment. Morgan offered to do the pictures for free, but the bride wouldn't hear of it.

"I will not have *any* of you working on my wedding day," she said. "As of today, you are all sisters in some way. So you'd better get used to having fun together!"

When they got to the church, Jade felt the nerves hit her all over again. She kept asking if there was anything she could do or if they'd forgotten anything. Her mom was the picture of coolness.

"Don't worry honey," she said, giving her a hug. "You head inside and relax. I've done this all before."

Jade laughed. "Is it easier the second time around?"

"Absolutely. Especially when you pick the right guy – nothing is easier."

Jade felt some tears pricking at her eyes, so she quickly kissed her mom on the cheek and got out of the car. She joined her sisters – all *three* of them – in their seats at the front.

The church was packed – almost every one of the 150 guests that were invited made the trip to the island for the wedding. Jade was touched by this; it showed how dearly loved the couple was, and didn't make it feel like a "second wedding" at all. It was a real wedding, full of real, honest to goodness love.

Chief Hank arrived and stood himself at the front of the church, shifting from foot to foot. Jade had never seen him dressed up before, and he looked quite dashing in his traditional black suit. For weeks, Morgan tried to convince him to wear a leopard print pocket square, but he opted for the classier champagne option. Jade thought it was the right choice, as funny as Morgan was being about it.

A few moments later, the delicate sounds of a piano playing *Here Comes the Bride* rang through the church. Jade felt the tightness in her throat; she snapped a quick picture with her phone of everyone standing and waiting for her mom to come down the aisle.

As soon as she appeared, Jade turned around to take a peek at Chief Hank. He was grinning from ear to ear and finally stopped swaying. And it looked like, just *maybe*, there was a mist in his eyes.

Jade turned back around to watch Connor and her mom walk gracefully down the aisle; she had to resist the urge to snap another picture. The photographer promised not to miss anything, and Jade reminded herself to just enjoy the moment.

Her mom chose the *perfect* dress – satin, with a scoop neck and a beautiful champagne coloring. It gave her a beautiful hourglass shape, and stopped at the ankle, giving her a glamorous 1950s look. Totally classy, and totally herself.

Jade managed to keep herself together for the ceremony, which she thought went too fast, and helped herd the guests onto the trolleys bound for Saltwater Cove. They hung back to get a few pictures in the church, but neither her mom nor Chief Hank had much patience for standing around.

"Alright everyone," said Chief Hank after fifteen minutes of posing. "We're too old to waste any more time getting our pictures taken. Let's get to the party!"

Chief Hank sent the photographer on her way so that their families could have a private ride back to the reception.

"Listen up," he said as the trolley pulled out of the parking lot. "Like it or not, we're all family now."

"A moment of silence," added Morgan, "for the peaceful lives you may have led. That's over from this moment on."

Everyone laughed.

Jade's mom interjected, "That's not true!"

"No," said Amanda. "Things will just be a bit...different."

Jade smiled. She'd been thinking about this a lot. As challenging as it could be to bring two families together, Jade thought it was an overwhelmingly positive thing.

She wanted to say something; she cleared her throat. "Yeah, it'll be different. Crazier, bigger, and louder. But also more full of joy and..."

Hm, what did she want to say again? Everyone was looking at her.

Jacob put a hand on her shoulder. "Go ahead, sis."

She smiled. "Without getting yelled at for being too cheesy, I wanted to say – I'm grateful for every one of you."

The trolley erupted into "aw's" and hugs. Jade hadn't intended to speak up, but she was glad she did. She even got a hug from Amanda. When they got to the barn, her mom stood up at the front to say one last thing.

"I love you all. Now let's have some fun!"

Introduction to *Saltwater Secrets*

Life on San Juan Island isn't always as idyllic as it seems...

Jade Clifton is more than ready for a fresh start. Finally free of her emotionally abusive ex, she's sure everything is about to get better for her. Except...it doesn't. A series of personal attacks on her property has her on edge, and Jade knows that she'll need help figuring out who is targeting her and why. She just never expected a certain sweet, ridiculously handsome sheriff's deputy to come to her rescue...

Matthew Stevens takes his job very seriously. He lives to protect and serve. But keeping Jade safe is more than just a job—it's personal. After months in the friend zone, he's starting to think she's the one for him and that they could be happy together. Now all he'll have to do is keep her safe long enough to convince her of that...

Secrets, rivals, and lies stand in their way. Can Jade and Matthew overcome it all and finally find their way to happily ever after?

Saltwater Secrets is book 3 in the Westcott Bay sweet and wholesome series. The series is best read in order. It features a shy heroine who is stronger than she realizes and a stern-but-sweet cop unraveling a small town mystery together. HEA guaranteed. Get your copy and start binge reading on Amazon today!

Would you like to join my reader group?

Sign up for my reader newsletter and get a free copy of my novella *Christmas at Saltwater Cove*. You can sign up by visiting: https://bit.ly/XmasSWC

About the Author

Amelia Addler writes always clean, always swoon-worthy romance stories and believes that everyone deserves their own happily ever after.

Her soulmate is a man who once spent five weeks driving her to work at 4AM after her car broke down (and he didn't complain, not even once). She is lucky enough to be married to that man and they live in Pittsburgh with their little yellow mutt. Visit her website at AmeliaAddler.com or drop her an email at amelia@AmeliaAddler.com.

Also by Amelia...

The Westcott Bay Series

Saltwater Cove

Saltwater Studios

Saltwater Secrets

Saltwater Crossing

Saltwater Falls

Saltwater Memories

Saltwater Promises

Christmas at Saltwater Cove

The Orcas Island Series

Sunset Cove

The Billionaire Date Series

Nurse's Date with a Billionaire

Doctor's Date with a Billionaire

Veterinarian's Date with a Billionaire